A Candlelight Ecstasy Romance®

"THIS ISLAND IS CHALLENGING, CLEO. KIND OF LIKE YOU."

Cleo looked away, embarrassed. "You're seeing challenges where none exist, Joe. Just because I'm not ruled by my emotions—"

"I'm surprised you'll admit you have any emotions, you try so hard to deny them. What happened to you, Cleo? You were never easy to understand, but now you're completely sealed off. It's like you feel threatened if anyone gets too close."

" 'Anyone' meaning you?" Suddenly she felt cold. "Don't flatter yourself, Joe. You're assuming I'm hiding something—"

"Assuming! I *know* you are, Cleo. And before we leave this island, I intend to find out what it is."

CANDLELIGHT ECSTASY CLASSIC ROMANCES

CANDLELIGHT ECSTASY ROMANCES®

CLEO'S TREASURE

Rose Marie Ferris

A CANDLELIGHT ECSTASY ROMANCE®

Published by
Dell Publishing Co., Inc.
1 Dag Hammarskjold Plaza
New York, New York 10017

Dell ® TM 681510, Dell Publishing Co., Inc.

Candlelight Ecstasy Romance®, 1,203,540, is a registered trademark of Dell Publishing Co., Inc., New York, New York.

ISBN: 0-440-11294-X

Printed in the United States of America

June 1987

10 9 8 7 6 5 4 3 2 1

WFH

To Our Readers:

We have been delighted with your enthusiastic response to Candlelight Ecstasy Romances®, and we thank you for the interest you have shown in this exciting series.

In the upcoming months we will continue to present the distinctive sensuous love stories you have come to expect only from Ecstasy. We look forward to bringing you many more books from your favorite authors and also the very finest work from new authors of contemporary romantic fiction.

As always, we are striving to present the unique, absorbing love stories that you enjoy most—books that are more than ordinary romance. Your suggestions and comments are always welcome. Please write to us at the address below.

Sincerely,

The Editors
Candlelight Romances
1 Dag Hammarskjold Plaza
New York, New York 10017

CLEO'S TREASURE

PROLOGUE

Excerpts from Elspeth Jarman's scrapbook:

Santa Rosa *Chronicle*, October 10, 1965.
THREE FEARED DEAD IN BOATING MISHAP
The gale force winds that ripped the northern California coast last weekend may have claimed three more victims. Coast Guard sources say the search continues for the *Fair Wind*, a 30-foot ocean cruiser with a crew of three, missing en route from Chelsea Island to Sausalito. The *Fair Wind* is owned by Roger Dennis, lead guitarist with the rock group Era . . .

Inside Publishing, "Critic's Corner," November, 1966.
. . . The latest, and tackiest, in the series of sexploitation books, *Rivals*, is a thinly disguised biography of rock star Roger Dennis. Penned by Dennis's widow, Suzanne Jarman, this opus scratches in public prurient itches that once were scratched only in private. One of the more bizarre chapters focuses on the "love trio" composed of Jarman, Dennis, and the "mystery woman" who delivers roses each month to Dennis's grave . . .

Santa Rosa *Chronicle,* June 13, 1967.

JURY HEARS ABOUT SEX ON PARK BENCH

Trial began Monday in a civil suit in Sonoma County Circuit Court filed by Adelaide Dennis, mother of Roger Dennis, the rock musician who died in a boating accident in October, 1965. Citing a recent centerfold in a popular men's magazine and the best-selling fictionalized biography of her son, Mrs. Dennis contends that her daughter-in-law, Suzanne Jarman, "leads a promiscuous and self-indulgent life," which makes her an unfit mother, and seeks custody of her granddaughter, Cleo Dennis, age seven.

In opening statements to the jury, lawyers in the case presented widely divergent views of Roger Dennis's marriage to Suzanne Jarman, but both agreed that the trial would be laden with graphic testimony detailing the couple's extramarital affairs. "They have pictures of Suzy Jarman making it with some guy on a park bench," said one juror, who asked to be excused. "I can't sit through weeks of this. One day was embarrassing enough."

Ms. Jarman has filed a countersuit for $200,000, claiming Mrs. Dennis's "scurrilous attacks have held me up to public ridicule, done irreparable harm to my reputation, and damaged my acting career." A spokesperson for Ms. Jarman told this reporter, "Suzanne feels no personal animosity toward Roger's mother. Being a mother herself, she appreciates the trauma of losing one's only child. She understands Adelaide's grief very well."

Mrs. Dennis was unavailable for comment . . .

People, May 2, 1974.

PEACE AT ANY PRICE?

What's it like being the most photographed woman in the country? "Not so great," says the shutterbug's darling, Suzanne Jarman. In a recent interview, she said, "I never wanted all this attention, but as long as doing interviews and photo layouts pays my legal fees, I'll close my eyes and think of the money."

Publicity has brought Suzanne more than financial rewards. "It's given me confidence, knowing I have thousands of allies out there. If the public believes my daughter belongs with me, perhaps public opinion will sway the judge."

This Wednesday, a California district court judge will announce his decision in Ms. Jarman's most recent appeal. If the court rules in her favor, what's next on La Jarman's agenda? "I have a movie commitment this summer," she says. "I'm playing myself in the screen adaptation of *Rivals.* After that, I just want to be left in peace with Cleo."

CHAPTER ONE

The man was gone when Cleo left the gallery. Had she only imagined he was following her?

She rattled the knob to make sure the door had locked, then peered into the gallery window as if she were admiring the seascape displayed there. In reality, she was studying the wedge of sidewalk and street and blue April sky reflected in the glass.

The man's Dodge van was gone, too, its place at the curb occupied by a sleek, silver-gray BMW.

Content that no prying eyes were watching, Cleo turned away from the window and ducked around the corner of the building, out of sight of the street.

In the last few days she had spotted the stranger half a dozen times: at the bank, the post office, the library, the service station, the supermarket, the coffee shop where she'd had a late breakfast this morning. Could coincidence explain that many encounters? Could she have seen more than one man?

No, Cleo decided. Not in a million years. As she hurried along the brick-paved alley toward her second-floor apartment, she acknowledged that somewhere in the world the stranger might have a double. Even a town as small as Mendocino had its share of unsavory creeps. But there couldn't be another aloha shirt like his; not this far from Waikiki.

In her worst nightmare, she could not have imagined that shirt. Nor was she imagining the very different sort of man who had stationed himself at the top of the stairway leading to her apartment.

Instead of ill-fitting slacks and a loud sports shirt, this man wore jeans and a crew-neck sweater, topped by a herringbone tweed jacket. Lithe and long-legged, with a lean athletic build, he had crisp black hair, the face of an amiable brigand, and a smile Cleo might have called irresistible if she'd found the tall, dark, dangerous type a turn-on.

In the few seconds it took her to reach the stairs, she summed up the stranger and dismissed him with one brief, assessing glance. Early thirties, she thought. Self-assured. Perhaps even arrogant. Attractive, certainly, but since she was immune to brigands, relatively harmless.

It never occurred to her that there might be some connection between this man and the stranger who had been following her.

"Looking for someone?" she inquired.

"Cleo?" Laugh lines crinkled the corners of his bold, black eyes. "You are Cleo Dennis, aren't you?"

The hint of mockery in his voice seemed familiar, as did the sardonic lift of his eyebrows and the way he cocked his head to one side and looked her over, from the toes of her sneakers to her windblown honey brown hair.

Cleo paused on the bottom step, looking up at him, one hand shading her eyes against the sun.

"Do I know you?" she asked.

He laughed outright, amused by her confusion, and in that moment Cleo recognized him.

14

"Joe Gamble," she said.

She hadn't seen him since the summer she'd spent at Chelsea almost twelve years ago, but she would know that laughter anywhere, that easy charm he put on and took off as effortlessly as if it were a hat. Joe had seldom displayed his charm for her, however. He had laughed at her, baited her, teased and challenged her.

"You don't seem pleased to see me, Cleo."

"Should I be?"

"Not necessarily, but after all this time I thought you might've stopped pretending you don't like me."

"What makes you think I'm pretending?"

"C'mon, Cleo. You can drop the act with me. That's what old friends are for."

"We were never friends, Joe."

"Maybe not, but you can't deny you had a crush on me."

Cleo resumed climbing the stairs. "What if I did? I was fourteen years old. Everyone's entitled to make a few mistakes at that age."

Undaunted, Joe leaned against the railing at his back and crossed one ankle over the other. "Your feelings for me may have changed, but some things haven't. You've still got that chip on your shoulder."

That's safer than my heart on my sleeve, Cleo thought. She bit her lip, striving for composure. She prided herself on the ability to control her emotions, but with Joe self-discipline seemed to slip away.

"Look," she said, "it's been a brutal day and I'm too tired to spar with you. You want politeness? Okay. I'll pretend I'm delighted to see you—"

"Don't bother. I prefer frankness."

"At least we agree on that."

She dug her latchkey out of the pocket of her shorts and unlocked the door, and Joe followed her inside without waiting for an invitation. He stood in the entry to the living area while she opened the windows overlooking the Pacific to let in the unseasonably warm evening breeze.

The room was furnished with linen-upholstered Scandinavian pieces sparsely distributed upon a gleaming hardwood floor. A triptych of California wildflowers—purple lupine, yellow azaleas, and orange poppies—drew the eye and provided the only touch of color aside from the pale splashes of sunlight that dappled the walls.

The decor underscored Cleo's break with the past. Yet she had stayed on the coast, less than a hundred miles from home, which implied the break was not complete. Not yet, Joe thought. He nodded to himself, encouraged by what he had learned about her.

"Mind if I sit down?" he said.

Cleo shrugged. "As long as you're here, you might as well be comfortable."

She dropped her keys into a smoked-glass bowl on the coffee table and perched on the edge of a club chair, facing him. Now that she'd had a few minutes to recover from the shock of seeing Joe Gamble, there were a number of questions she needed to resolve, beginning with the one that was foremost in her mind.

"How did you find me?" she asked.

"It wasn't easy. It took two months and a lot of shoe leather. I gather you didn't want to be found."

"Not by the press."

"Don't worry. I'm not a reporter. Your secret's safe with me."

Cleo frowned and brushed nonexistent dust off the already shining table. Joe didn't understand. He couldn't.

16

No one could, unless, like her, they had been hounded by the news media.

The torturous process of suit-countersuit had been over for more than a decade. The legal maneuvers had ended with the supper-club fire that took her mother's life. A few years later, when Cleo was eighteen, her grandmother, Adelaide Dennis, had died. But interest in these strong-willed women persisted.

The public, it seemed, had an insatiable appetite for gossip—the juicier, the better. Even now, years after her death, a certain type of reader wanted to know everything there was to know about Suzanne Jarman. They wanted to know about her ill-fated marriage to Roger Dennis and her relationship with her daughter, but they were most curious about her bitter rivalry with Adelaide Dennis and her battle with Adelaide for Cleo's custody. And even now, from time to time, some ambitious, unprincipled newsman would track Cleo down and attempt to revive the scandal.

This meant she had no secrets. No matter how carefully she chose her acquaintances or how discreetly she lived, she had only the illusion of privacy.

She met Joe's gaze, her gray eyes clouded with skepticism. "If you're not a reporter, why did you waste your time and shoe leather looking for me?"

"I promised your great-aunt I'd locate you."

A tinge of pink washed over Cleo's cheekbones, but she did not look away. "I know how fond you were of Elspeth," she said softly. "I was sorry to hear of her death."

"Who told you about it?"

"The editor of the Mendocino *Courier*. He wanted to run a feature on her and he asked for my reaction."

17

"Did you tell him to go chase himself?"

"No, I told him the same thing I told you. That I'm sorry she's gone."

"But not sorry enough to come to the funeral," said Joe.

"I sent flowers. Wait a minute—is that how you found me? Through the florist?"

Joe ignored her question. "Sending flowers isn't the same as paying your respects in person, Cleo."

"How I paid my respects is none of your business, Joe. Besides, Aunt Elspeth and I weren't particularly close."

"You might've been, if you'd given her half a chance."

"You don't know what you're talking about. In the four years I was at school in Sonoma, I might as well have been on the dark side of the moon. Aunt Elspeth never once came to see me."

"You can thank Addie Dennis's trained judge for that. She got him to issue a restraining order." Scowling, Joe got to his feet and crossed the room to stand directly in front of Cleo. He was so close the rough denim of his jeans grazed her knees; so close she could feel the heat radiating from his body and sense the coldness of his contempt.

"Admit it," he said. "You couldn't be bothered to keep in touch, so you assumed your aunt wouldn't give a damn if she never heard from you again. But the fact is, she did care—more than you deserve. She worried about you constantly, and she felt a certain obligation to you. She was terribly conscious that she was the last of your mother's family, the last of the California Jarmans. God knows why, but she'd have given anything to see you."

Imprisoned in her chair, Cleo felt breathless and claustrophobic. Her first impulse was to pull away from Joe, to huddle deeper into the upholstery and put some small distance between them. But she refused to let him see that he'd intimidated her. Even when he braced his hands on the chair arms and leaned over her, she sat perfectly still, her face impassive.

She kept her eyes fixed on his chest, on the weave of his cable-knit sweater and the pattern of pewter and charcoal chevrons in his lapel as she said, "I'm not a mind reader, Joe. If you're trying to lay a guilt trip on me, it won't work. I had no idea Aunt Elspeth wanted to see me."

Joe grasped her chin and forced her head back so that she had to look at him. "If you'd known, would it have made any difference?"

"Probably not."

Startled by her defiance, he let go of her chin. He swung away from her and strode toward the windows, muttering, "You're your own worst enemy, Cleo Dennis, but at least you're honest."

"And you resent it."

"You bet I do." He sounded resigned, yet exasperated, and when he turned to face her his expression was as accusing as his voice. "Elspeth Jarman deserved more than a spray of camellias from you. Damn it, Cleo! You of all people should know that."

He's right, she thought. I should know. But that didn't make Joe's criticism any more palatable.

Torn between anger and irony, she rose and walked to the front door and opened it.

"I'd like you to leave now," she said. "I've told you I'm sorry. There's nothing more I can do."

"I wouldn't be too sure of that, Cleo. If you're game, you could help fulfill your aunt's last request."

19

"If I'm game?" Cleo stared at him, mystified. "What would I have to do?"

"Nothing felonious," he replied dryly. "Come sit down and I'll tell you about it."

He sat on the sofa, and realizing that he had no intention of leaving, Cleo returned, somewhat warily, to her chair. "If this 'last request' is one of Aunt Elspeth's schemes, I'm not sure I want to get involved."

Joe chuckled. "I take it you remember how eccentric she was."

"Of course I do. She wasn't the sort of person one forgets."

"No, she wasn't," said Joe.

Surprised by a wave of nostalgia, Cleo relaxed and curled up in her chair. "I always associated Aunt Elspeth with color and movement. Everything about her, everything she did, seemed exaggerated, larger than life. The way she dressed, the language she used, the way she'd laugh and gesture with her hands—it was as if she were always on stage."

"Did you know she actually was a Ziegfeld Girl?"

Cleo nodded. "She told me about her run on Broadway I don't know how many times, but I didn't believe her. At least, not at first. I mean, here was this caricature of a flapper, in her bobbed wig and rolled stockings and endless strands of beads."

"I don't think she bought any clothes after the shimmy dress went out of style," said Joe. "She never stopped reliving her glory years."

"I realize that now, but at the time I wasn't perceptive enough to figure her out. All I knew was that she was full of stories about the big events of the twenties."

"She was a habitual name-dropper too," said Joe.

"When she got cranked up, she sounded like the talking edition of *Who's Who.*"

"I know exactly what you mean," said Cleo. "To hear her tell it, she'd been a personal friend to all sorts of celebrities, from Charlie Chaplin to Rudolph Valentino. And half of them wanted to marry her! But to me, she looked like an overage Lorelei Lee. I was never sure what was fact and what was fantasy, till one day when I was messing around in the attic and I came across one of her scrapbooks literally stuffed with reviews and theater programs and dance cards."

"Was there a pressed rose and a note from Noel Coward?"

"That's the one," said Cleo. "And that's when I realized Aunt Elspeth hadn't fabricated the whole thing."

Joe grinned and lounged back against the upholstery, his hands behind his head. "What else do you remember about Elspeth, Cleo?"

"Well, I remember her predicting you'd go far if you could overcome your natural tendency toward sloth." Still grinning, Joe threw one of the sofa pillows at Cleo. She resisted the impulse to throw it back and instead held it on her lap, absently smoothing her hands over the nubby texture of the pillow sham as she added, "She also used to say that your Achilles' heel was that you couldn't refuse a dare."

"That's funny," Joe replied quietly. "She said just the opposite about you."

"Did she really?"

"Honest to God. She said the willingness to take risks would be your salvation."

Cleo averted her gaze, hiding the eagerness in her eyes

21

as she inquired, "Did my aunt say anything else about me?"

"Uh-huh. She said you'd inherited your father's eyes, your mother's passion, and your grandmother's stubbornness. But your nose, she said, was strictly your own."

Cleo self-consciously touched her nose, tracing its impudent tip with one finger. Then, squaring her shoulders, she declared, "My aunt was right about that, Joe Gamble, and I do my damnedest to keep it that way."

"Meaning?"

"Meaning I don't poke my nose into other people's business, and I appreciate it when others return the courtesy."

"Is that why you think I came here? To snoop?"

"Didn't you?"

"Sorry to disappoint you, Cleo, but I've got better things to do than spy on you. I wouldn't be here right now if I hadn't promised Elspeth I'd contact you."

Joe hadn't raised his voice, but Cleo sensed his indignation. She saw it in the intense stillness that had stolen over him. She clasped her hands together to steady them as she said, "Then there really is a last request."

"Absolutely."

"What is it?"

Joe swung his feet to the floor and hauled himself erect. "It's difficult to explain, but what it boils down to is that Elspeth wanted you to attend a get-together she organized for her surviving relatives."

"I thought I was her only relative."

"You're not," said Joe. "You have some distant cousins in Ohio."

"And they're coming to this get-together?"

22

"They wouldn't miss it. In fact, they're due to arrive at the island this weekend."

Cleo knitted her brows. "It doesn't make sense, Joe. Why would these long lost cousins travel all the way from Ohio just to attend a wake?"

"Who said anything about a wake? This shindig is more elaborate than that. It's more like—well, I guess you could call it a house party." After a momentary hesitation, Joe added, "Then, too, there is an extra inducement . . ." He lapsed into silence, realizing that Cleo had stopped listening.

In her mind's eye, she could see the main lodge on Chelsea, rising like a fortress from the top of its hill. With its three stories of stone and weathered shingles girdled by verandas, flanked by pillars, and surmounted by a white-railed widow's walk, the outside of the house might have inspired the cover art for a Gothic novel. The rooms inside were cavernous and drafty, but the sweeping balustrades and beveled-glass windows, the glowing tapestries, onyx mantelpieces, and chandeliers dripping crystal prisms revealed the split personality of the place.

On first seeing the lodge the summer she was fourteen, Cleo understood why her great-grandfather had been nicknamed "Crazy" Jarman. Only a madman would have tried to mix nineteenth-century elegance with Victorian angst. But as the summer progressed and she saw the rooms filled with light and flowers and music and laughter, she formed a grudging attachment to the place.

That fall, enrolled at a boarding school thirty miles inland, she had longed for the topsy-turvy ambiance of the island. She had missed her aunt. But most of all, she had missed Joe. . . .

"So there'll be guests at Chelsea again," she murmured.

"That's right," Joe replied. "Six of us—seven, if you decide to join the party."

"How long will you be staying?"

"Ten days."

From Cleo's horrified expression, he might have said ten years. He wasn't handling this at all well. Charm hadn't worked. Neither had outrage or sentiment. His final recourse was persuasion. Knowing that, he should have taken time to prepare her, to lay the groundwork so that she couldn't refuse. With anyone else he would have, but Cleo kept him off balance. Always had.

She baffled and disturbed him. She was contradictory, a riddle with a go-to-hell glint in her quicksilver eyes, a generous mouth, a turned up nose, and smooth, creamy skin his hands ached to touch.

When she was a kid, he hadn't known whether to paddle her or kiss her, and he was dismayed to find that he still wasn't sure how to deal with her. What's more, he was afraid she knew it. She was looking at him as if she could see straight through him and didn't much like what she saw.

His only option was to play his ace in the hole and hope to hell it succeeded.

He withdrew a sealed manila envelope from his inside jacket pocket and dropped it on the coffee table. "Elspeth recorded a cassette for you. I haven't listened to it, but it should answer any questions you have."

The color drained from Cleo's face. She made no move to pick up the envelope.

"There's no need to settle this tonight," he said. "Take your time. Think it over. I'll be at the Breakers Motel till

Friday. You can call me there and let me know what you decide." He paused, giving Cleo the chance to comment, but she remained silent until he started toward the door.

Hurrying after him, she said, "I don't need to think about it, Joe. In case it's escaped your notice, I have a business to run. I can't just abandon it."

"The gallery's not open till the end of May," he countered. "I saw the sign in the window."

"Even so, there are loads of things I have to take care of before the tourist season begins. That's assuming I *wanted* to spend ten days at Chelsea."

"Don't be too hasty, Cleo. There are advantages."

"Name one."

"Well, you wouldn't have to worry about reporters on the island." Joe saw that she was weakening. "You'd also get to meet your cousins," he added.

Her rueful smile made him wish he'd quit while he was ahead.

"I've never had much luck with relatives, Joe."

"Maybe your luck's changed for the better."

"And maybe it hasn't."

She looked so dejected he wanted to comfort her. He touched his knuckles to the point of her jaw in a familiar "chin up" gesture, but when he reached out to hold her, she eluded his arms and stepped through the open door.

Sighing, silently cursing himself for behaving like the worst kind of fool, Joe followed her onto the landing. "I hate to belabor the issue," he said, "but this visit to Chelsea is your aunt's last request. And as I said before, there is another inducement."

"What is it?" Cleo inquired, her voice distant and cool.

"Just one of Elspeth's flakier ideas," Joe replied in a

25

lazy drawl, stringing her along. "You probably won't be interested."

"You'll never know unless you try me."

The flicker of curiosity in the misty depths of Cleo's eyes told Joe she was intrigued. He grinned, pleased by this small success. "Would you believe, a treasure hunt?" he said.

CHAPTER TWO

A treasure hunt? The idea was preposterous, farcical, absurd—and utterly typical of Elspeth Jarman.

"I can believe Aunt Elspeth arranged a hunt," Cleo said, "but I don't believe there's a treasure."

"You didn't believe you have other relatives either," Joe argued, "yet I'm here to tell you, you do."

Cleo shook her head, discounting his logic. She leaned against the handrail and concentrated on the view of rooftops and horizon, on the brilliant coral sun dipping into the cobalt sea as she said, "According to the local paper, Aunt Elspeth deeded Chelsea over to some kind of historical society."

"The Native Sons of the Golden West," said Joe. "In return for her donation, they paid the taxes on the property and guaranteed Elspeth a life estate."

"That proves there's no treasure. If she'd had any assets, she'd never have given up ownership of the island."

"You may be right," Joe said. "Then again, you never know. Elspeth had a houseful of personal belongings."

"But she sold everything of value years ago to defray my mother's legal expenses and bankroll her movies—"

"You don't have to draw me a diagram, Cleo. I'll concede Elspeth had no head for business. She was the first

27

to admit she lost a bundle on *Rivals* alone. But like I said, the treasure hunt's an extra. I only mentioned it because nothing else seemed to work."

"So you thought the possibility of financial gain might appeal to my mercenary instincts."

"That's about the size of it," Joe agreed.

Cleo stole a sidelong glance at him. "Emotional blackmail won't work either."

"No?" With an idle forefinger, Joe traced a tingling path along her forearm, from wrist to elbow, elbow to wrist. "How about seduction?" he asked.

She didn't take him seriously. How could she, when she heard laughter in his voice? But suddenly, she was trembling. Drawing herself to her full height, she said, "Don't do me any favors, Joe. You've made your pitch. Now give me a chance to think it over."

Joe pushed himself away from the handrail and shrugged, as if to say, "it was worth a try." He ran down the stairs without a backward glance, and as he walked toward the street, the swagger in his step told Cleo his ego was unbruised. At the mouth of the alley, he turned to look at her.

"Call me," he said. "Let me know what you decide."

Don't wait, urged an inner voice. *Give him your answer tonight. Last request or not, tell him exactly what he can do with his charm and his arrogance and his proposition.*

Cleo was tempted to respond with an unqualified *no,* but something made her hesitate. "I'll be in touch," she said.

She watched Joe leave, certain she would not be returning to Chelsea with him. But less than an hour later, she had begun to reconsider.

She listened to her aunt's cassette tape, expecting expressions of regret and affection, resolving not to be swayed by cheap sentiment. She was not prepared for Elspeth's matter-of-fact approach or for the snapshot her aunt had enclosed.

The photograph showed Cleo at her adolescent worst, coltish and sullen, wearing rolled up blue jeans and a faded T-shirt, frowning into the camera. After a hasty look at the picture, she put it aside and sat down to listen to the cassette.

"By the time you hear this," Elspeth began in a crisp, no-nonsense tone, "Joe will have told you about the get-together I've planned, and you will have decided you want no part of it. To be honest, Cleo, I don't blame you. If I were you, I'd feel the same way. This tape may be a waste of my time and yours. It may be that nothing I can say will change your mind. Still, I have to try.

"I've always been an optimist, you see, but in the last few months my optimism has been tempered by acceptance of my own mortality. I've seen so many specialists, the combined initials of their advance degrees would make enough alphabet soup to feed an army. I've been probed, punctured, and scanned, and the prognosis is unanimous. I haven't long to live. At my age, that's not surprising. What is surprising is that I find the prospect of death less worrisome than the realization that this is my last chance to arrange a meeting between you and your cousins. Thanks to Joe, the Ohio Jarmans have agreed to attend my house party, which leaves only one problem: How do I persuade you to come?

"I've given this a good deal of thought, my dear. I could tell you I love you and base my appeal on that. But what reason have you to believe me? And if you believed me, why should you indulge an old lady's whim?

"I ask myself this, aware that, whether they intended to or not, your mother and your grandmother deprived you of your heritage and destroyed any sense of kinship you might have had with either the Jarmans or the Dennises. My sorrow—the sorrow that haunts me, the one I shall carry to my grave—is that I never lifted a finger to stop Suzanne and Addie. With one exception.

"Do you remember that occasion as clearly as I do, Cleo? I pray you do, and that you remember the promise you gave me as well. If you remember, you'll join the house party. If you've forgotten, if this recording doesn't jog your memory, there is nothing more I can say."

Reminders weren't necessary. Cleo recalled the incident Elspeth referred to. She doubted she would ever forget the day, shortly after her arrival at Chelsea, when she had approached her great-aunt in tears and begged Elspeth to intercede with Suzanne in her behalf.

"My mother wants me to go to L.A. with her," she'd sobbed, "and I hate it there. There's nothing to do but hang around the back lot."

Elspeth had offered sympathy and a delicate square of lace-edged linen that smelled of jasmine. "Hush, child. Dry your tears and look at the bright side. If you go to Los Angeles, you'll get to see more of Suzanne."

"No, I won't. She'll be so busy with her movie, she won't have time for me. I want to stay here."

Elspeth bowed her head. For a while she sat in thoughtful silence. Only the creak of her rocking chair and the gentle pushing of her toes against the bleached floorboards of the veranda disturbed the stillness of the summer afternoon. Just when Cleo thought the old lady must have dozed off, she said, "Does this sudden desire

30

to prolong your visit have anything to do with Joe Gamble?"

Too flustered to answer, Cleo blushed and looked away.

"Have you told your mother how you feel?"

"I've tried to, Aunt Elspeth. I've tried and tried to talk to her, but she only laughs and says Joe's a phase I'm going through."

"Would you like me to speak to her?"

Cleo stared at her great-aunt, her eyes wide and imploring. "Would you do that for me?"

"Are you sure you want to stay?"

"I do. Truly I do—more than anything!"

The tempo of Elspeth's rocking quickened. "Then I'll speak to Suzanne."

Elspeth had kept her word. She had spoken to Suzanne that very evening. Cleo listened through the heating register in her bedroom while, with uncanny insight, Elspeth explained her feelings for Joe.

But Suzanne was unmoved. "Don't overdramatize this thing," she responded lightly, "and don't dignify a teenage crush by calling it love. Cleo's a baby."

"She's fourteen, Suzy. When you were her age, you'd fallen in and out of love a dozen times or more."

"That's precisely the point, Aunt Elspeth. Joe's the first boy Cleo's been attracted to. Next week she'll meet someone else and wonder what she ever saw in him."

"That's where you're mistaken, my dear. Cleo's not the fickle type. Her feelings go too deep." A ripple of laughter drifted through the open vent, and Elspeth continued querulously, chiding Suzanne. "I'm glad you find this humorous. I see nothing funny about it myself."

"Well, what do you expect? Cleo fancies she has this

31

undying passion for Joe. That much is understandable and completely natural. He's quite dishy, after all. But I can't take it seriously, and if you do, then I'm afraid you're getting dotty in your old age."

"Dotty, is it? Let me tell you, Suzanne Jarman, I'd rather be a dotty old woman than a hard-boiled young one!"

"Hogwash! You'd rather be young than anything."

"Perhaps you're right about me, but you're wrong about your daughter." Elspeth punctuated her retort with an indignant thump of her cane. "Mark my words, Suzanne. The flower of passion blooms free and wild. In the mind of a scholar, the soul of a gypsy, the heart of a child—"

"Oh, for pity's sake! That does it. I give up."

Now it was Elspeth who laughed. "Can I assume you've decided to let Cleo stay with me when the movie company goes on to L.A.?"

"You can assume whatever you like, only please, *please*, spare me your dreadful rhymes."

"Hmmph!" Elspeth snorted. "Some people have no taste."

"And some have no talent."

"And some have no tact."

In the long, uneasy silence that followed this spat, Cleo rolled onto her stomach and pressed her cheek against the grating. Dust from the ancient heating pipes made her nose itch and her eyes water, but if she listened for all she was worth, she could make out the sound of ice cubes being dropped into a glass and the faint chink of crystal against crystal as one of the women in the parlor below her, probably her mother, poured a drink.

When Suzanne spoke again, a note of resignation soft-ened her voice. "Maybe it's for the best," she said.

"What, dear?"

"Cleo's staying here. The more she sees of Joe, the sooner she'll get over this ridiculous case of puppy love. And, Aunt Elspeth, I'm relying on you to keep Addie Dennis from getting wind of this. My God! She'd pitch a fit if she knew her precious granddaughter was smitten with the son of a common servant."

"Mrs. Gamble supervises my home, Suzanne. She's no-body's servant and she happens to be one of the finest women I know. There is nothing common about her."

"That wouldn't cut any ice with Addie. It wouldn't score any points with the court either."

"Well, don't worry, dear. Mum's the word. Adelaide Dennis won't hear about any of this from me."

Suzanne took a sip of her drink, sighed, and mur-mured, "With any luck, by fall all of this will have blown over."

A sneeze caught Cleo unaware—and it wasn't a dainty, ladylike sneeze, but an explosive *ahchoo!* that reverber-ated through the heating pipes and echoed in the parlor.

"What was that?" said Suzanne.

Cleo pinched her nostrils and held her breath, but the urge to sneeze a second time was too powerful to sup-press, and this time her mother identified both the sneeze and its source.

"You've got your way, Cleo," she called. "But if you don't stop eavesdropping—and I mean this very instant —I might decide you're too big a handful for your great-aunt to cope with."

Suzanne had never been much of a disciplinarian. She might have been bluffing, but Cleo was not about to push

33

her luck. She closed the vent, loudly, so that Suzanne would know she hadn't dawdled.

That was the last of their conversation she overheard, but it was not the last time she eavesdropped.

The next morning she had apologized to her mother, and on the day Suzanne left for Hollywood, she'd thanked Elspeth for intervening.

"I'll repay you for this someday," she'd promised. "If there's ever anything you want me to do, all you have to do is ask."

And now someday had come and her great-aunt was asking.

Dusk had invaded the living room, but Cleo hardly noticed the fading light. With a pensive frown, she switched off the tape recorder and picked up the snapshot.

It had been taken at Treasure Bay, the isolated cove she had considered her secret hideaway. Even half hidden by the twilight the picture brought back memories of sun drenched days and starry nights and cookouts on the beach; of Joe surf-fishing while she explored the tide pools, of the sand castle they had built together one July afternoon, and her own intricately structured castles in the air.

In the weeks that followed her mother's departure, she had spent much of her time weaving daydreams about Joe Gamble. She had dogged his heels and bombarded him with questions and generally made a nuisance of herself, and when she discovered he was going steady with a girl he'd met at college, she hadn't been disheartened; she had loved him so fervently she never doubted that he must love her just a little.

In her fantasies, she had been magically transformed

into a creature of voluptuous allure, as glamorous as her mother. She'd become desirable, witty, sophisticated, and at least seventeen.

Joe was transformed too, although not in age or appearance. Even at fourteen, she'd known there were times when a person couldn't improve on nature, and in her daydreams she'd never tampered with Joe's lean young body or the austere beauty of his face. But his attitude toward her changed.

Instead of treating her with an amused tolerance, as if she were his pesky kid sister, in her fantasy he treated her like the woman she wished she could be. Instead of calling her "squirt" or "rowdy," he paid her extravagant compliments and called her "my lovely," "my princess," "my pearl."

Sometimes she imagined Joe saving her from a great disaster; an earthquake or a flood. Sometimes she saved him. But whatever the catastrophe, her makeup remained flawless and not a strand of her hair was out of place.

Sometimes she imagined they were shipwrecked, just the two of them cast up on some remote desolate shore, braving the elements and creating a paradise. And when a ship appeared on the horizon and rescue seemed imminent, Joe would gaze into her eyes and realize how beautiful she was and how much he adored her. He would douse the signal fire, fold her in his arms, and say, "I can't bear the thought of sharing you with others, my precious. I must have you to myself."

Cleo was not a precocious adolescent. Perhaps it was her grandmother's influence, or perhaps she was naturally modest, but at fourteen the mechanics of lovemaking seemed more comical than romantic. Besides, her understanding of the more intimate details of the sex act was hazy at best. Her daydreams invariably ended with Joe sweeping her off her feet and kissing her.

And then, on the first weekend in August, Joe's girlfriend, Steffi Haynes, paid a visit to the island and the dreams stopped altogether.

The moment she saw Steffi, Cleo knew why Joe found her appealing. Although she had been born and raised in Boulder, Colorado, she had the fresh-faced radiance of a California girl. And besides being strikingly pretty, Steffi was sweet. She was sugar and spice and everything nice, which meant it wasn't much fun hating her.

Seeing Joe with Steffi was sheer torture, but Cleo didn't let jealousy stop her from tagging along on their sightseeing expeditions. Wherever they went that weekend, she went too—until Sunday evening, when Joe and Steffi snuck away to a dance on the mainland while she was changing for dinner.

She went to bed early that night, consumed by envy because Steffi had everything she wanted for herself: blond hair, confidence, a gorgeous figure—and Joe. In the privacy of her bedroom she gave herself over to a storm of tears, and the intensity of her emotions left her exhausted. She was almost asleep when the murmur of voices from the parlor told her Joe and Steffi had returned.

They were speaking softly. Cleo could hear only snatches of their conversation, and now and again there was a silence, during which she envisioned them kissing. She dreaded those silences, and as they became longer and more frequent, she tried not to listen. But the occasional bits of dialogue she heard aroused her curiosity, and when Steffi said her name, Cleo climbed out of bed and tiptoed soundlessly across the room to the register.

36

She dropped to her knees and leaned close to the grating in time to hear Steffi say, "Don't be silly, Joe. I am not jealous. It's just that I've been looking forward to this weekend all summer. I missed you, bunny."

"Me too," Joe replied in a hoarse whisper. "So why are we wasting time talking about Cleo?"

"Maybe because this is the first moment we've had alone since Friday."

"So? What about it?"

"Cleo's like your shadow, Joe. Every time I turn around, there she is, looking at you with those big hungry eyes."

"Listen, Steffi, I know she has a crush on me—"

"It's more than a crush, Joe. It's an obsession."

"So what's your point? I haven't done anything to encourage her."

"You haven't *dis*couraged her either. She practically lives in your pocket, and you let her. And I want to know why."

"Aw, Steffi, have a heart. Forget about Cleo and concentrate on this."

"No, bunny. Please. We shouldn't—"

Whatever Joe had done to provoke Steffi's halfhearted protest, Cleo didn't believe Steffi wanted him to quit doing it, and judging by the rustling, sighing noises that came through the register, Joe didn't believe Steffi either. But soon the sighs turned to heavy breathing, and the whisper of clothing was replaced by a scuffle, which culminated in a slap.

"Stop it, Joe," Steffi panted. "I mean it. Keep your hands to yourself. We're not doing anything till you answer me."

"I haven't given it much thought," Joe grumbled. "All

I can tell you is, I don't want to hurt Cleo's feelings. She has enough problems without me adding to 'em."

"Are you sure you're not flattered by her interest?"

"Flattered? You've gotta be kidding."

"I'm not, Joe. The way she idolizes you must appeal to your ego."

"It doesn't. She's just a kid, Steffi. I figure she'll outgrow me."

"What am I supposed to do in the meantime?"

"Why don't we kiss and make up." Joe's voice deepened. "Honest, honey. I feel sorry for the little twerp, that's all."

Cleo had been living on hope, telling herself Joe cared for her, that someday he would realize how much. But in that moment of painful clarity, she knew she had been deluding herself.

He pitied her.

She crept back to bed and burrowed under the covers, where she lay staring into the darkness, dry-eyed, too heartsick to fall asleep, too mortified for tears. Sometime before dawn she vowed that she would never eavesdrop again. And never, under any circumstances, would she let Joe find out how deeply he had wounded her.

The next morning the pretense had begun. For the few remaining weeks of that long-ago summer, she had avoided Joe, and when she couldn't avoid him she'd acted as if he were her enemy.

There were times when she lashed out at him, and knowing that she had hurt him, she felt mean and petty and totally demoralized. But she hadn't relented. Her only excuse was pride and inexperience and the misguided notion that, if Joe were convinced he had lost her, he might see her in a new, romantic light.

He hadn't of course, and now she could laugh at her foolishness. Even if she had been blessed with Steffi Haynes's picture-book prettiness, she couldn't have overcome the gap between fourteen and nineteen.

In retrospect, in the comforting darkness of her living room, Cleo admitted how badly she had behaved. Joe hadn't led her on. His only crime had been not loving her, and it occurred to her that she owed him an apology.

And Elspeth, Cleo thought. I owe her, too. A debt of gratitude, of loyalty. An expression of affection more personal than a spray of camellias. Despite her idiosyncrasies, when the chips were down her great-aunt had come through for her, and Cleo felt she should pay homage, not because Elspeth had died, but for the way she'd lived.

But something inside her balked at the idea of spending ten days at Chelsea.

Ten days with Joe.

Seeing him had revived all the old insecurities and more than a little of the enchantment. The five years between them made much less difference than it had when she was fourteen, which left her feeling vulnerable. And confused.

Would proximity increase the attraction, or dispel it?

Cleo sensed she had reached a crossroads. One route was safe and familiar; the other filled with unknown perils. But it was infinitely more exciting. And just when the right choice seemed crucial, she had more questions than answers.

CHAPTER THREE

Joe found Cleo waiting outside his motel room on Friday morning. He stood in the doorway, zipping his wind-breaker against the dank ocean breeze, and when he saw the suitcases at Cleo's feet he grinned as if he'd never doubted that eventually she would see things his way.

"You've decided to join the treasure hunt," he said.

He was so sure of himself that Cleo experienced a vague stirring of irritation. "Yes," she replied, "but I have to tell you, I still don't believe there's a treasure."

"That doesn't matter. What's important is that you're coming with me."

Cleo wished he wouldn't stand so near. He smelled of shaving soap and toothpaste, his hair was slightly damp from the shower, and he looked vital and clear-eyed, ea-ger to tackle whatever problems the day might bring. By comparison, she felt wan and listless and uncomfortably aware that her appearance reflected two sleepless nights.

"Have you had breakfast?" he asked.

"Some toast. That's all I could manage."

"Don't worry, Cleo. You're doing the right thing."

"Then why do I have the feeling I'll regret it?"

She thought she saw compassion in Joe's eyes and turned away, but he only clapped her on the shoulder and picked up her suitcases. "C'mon, squirt," he said. "I'll buy you a cup of coffee."

The situation seemed less threatening once she was seated across from Joe in the motel coffee shop, perhaps because there was a table between them and she was no longer the object of his undivided attention. He laughed with the waitress and called her by name. He inquired about her children, and although he made no special requests, she brought him extra honey for his croissant and extra cream for his coffee.

Cleo marveled at the woman's cheerfulness. In the five years she had lived in Mendocino, she had never seen Becky Lee smile. In fact, she knew the waitress's name only because it was embroidered on her uniform, yet two days after Joe waltzed into town, Becky Lee acted as if he were an old and very dear friend. How does he do it? Cleo wondered, watching Joe dig into his scrambled eggs. He paused with his fork halfway to his mouth.

"Are you sure you don't want something to eat?"

"Just this," Cleo said, helping herself to the strawberry that garnished his plate.

Joe gave her one of his patented heart-melting grins. "I'd forgotten you're a food snitch."

She, on the other hand, had forgotten nothing about him. Not the shape of his ears or his long, beautifully formed fingers or his strong white teeth or the way he smothered almost everything he ate with ketchup. Pleased that she had snatched the strawberry out of harm's way, Cleo ate it slowly, savoring its springtime flavor, staring out the window at the clouds massing over the ocean.

"Looks like we might get rain," Joe remarked.

Cleo agreed.

"Are you planning on driving your own car down the coast?" he asked.

"If you've no objection, I'd rather ride with you. The only thing holding my car together is bumper stickers, and besides, there are some things I'd like to talk to you about."

"Such as?"

"I'd like to know more about the arrangements Aunt Elspeth made for this party, and I have some questions about my cousins." Joe nodded. Cleo stirred sugar into her coffee before she went on. "Then, too, you never did tell me how you found me."

"Sorry, Cleo. That's one question I can't answer. I'm not at liberty to divulge my sources."

The spoon rattled against the side of her cup. "What sources? What do you mean?"

In reply, Joe pulled his billfold out of his hip pocket and handed her a business card.

" 'G and G Associates, Investigations,' " Cleo read the engraving aloud. " 'Criminal, Civil, Insurance. Divorce, Child Custody, Missing Persons . . .' "

She faltered into silence; her gaze flew from the card to Joe.

"That's me," he said. "The missing persons specialist at G and G."

"Is this a joke?" she asked, her voice faint with surprise.

"Nope. I'm a private detective, bonded and state licensed. Want to see my badge?"

"That's not necessary. It's just that the last time I saw you, you were talking about becoming a lawyer."

"Wrong," said Joe. "I talked about becoming a skier.

42

Law school was supposed to pay the rent if the skiing didn't pan out."

"So what happened?"

"Neither one of 'em panned out. You know how it is, Cleo. When you're a kid you find something you like to do and you think, 'Boy, it'd be neat to make a career of this.' Then you get to doing it professionally, and pretty soon it's no fun anymore. It gets to be a grind."

"And that's why you gave up skiing?"

"I didn't give it up. Not entirely. Now that it's not my job, I enjoy skiing again."

Cleo twirled the strawberry stem, then put it in the ashtray. "What about law school?" she asked.

"I gave it a try, mostly to humor my mother. But I've never been much of a scholar. I mean, apart from the ski team, the only thing I liked about college was a criminology course I took in my senior year. So during the semester break, I put in an application with the San Francisco Police Department. After I got the job, I never looked back."

"Wasn't your mother disappointed that you dropped out?"

"Not really." Joe shrugged and added a dollop of ketchup to his hash browns. "Mom wanted me to know I had choices, and I guess she figured I'd learned that lesson."

Cleo studied Joe thoughtfully, trying to picture him as a detective. "How long were you with the police force?" she asked.

"Six years. About half that time I was a patrolman, and the other half I was with the vice squad. Then I got assigned to a bunco case where I was working as liaison with the Shore Patrol, and that's when I met my partner,

Stan Gleason. We didn't hit it off at first." Joe paused for a bite of hash browns. "Stan was career navy," he continued, shaking his head. "Everything by the book, spit and polish all the way, and I've always been more of a seat-of-the-pants detective. But by the time we wrapped up the case we realized how well we complemented each other. I have the instincts and Stan has the theory. I liked the action and hated the paperwork, and after thirty years in the military, Stan preferred desk duty, so when he retired a few months later, we decided to open our own agency."

"Is that what G and G stands for? Gamble and Gleason?"

"Or Gleason and Gamble," said Joe. "Stan and I couldn't agree on who should get top billing."

Joe's mention of billing touched on the issue of finances; a subject Cleo chose to approach with caution. "Do you and Stan disagree about many things?"

"Enough," Joe conceded, smiling. "Why do you ask?"

"I wondered if he approves of your devoting so much time to tracking down Aunt Elspeth's relatives."

Joe's expression didn't change, but a hint of impatience roughened his voice as he replied, "Unless I'm mistaken, Cleo, that's your subtle way of asking what's in this for me."

"I didn't want to put it so crudely, but as long as you've brought the subject up, your agency must charge some sort of fee."

"It does. In cases like this, the standard fee is thirty percent of the appraised value of the inheritance."

"With the heir picking up the tab?"

"Somebody has to cover expenses," said Joe. "We're in business to make a profit, but our clients profit too."

"What happens if an estate has no value?"

Joe stood up and slapped some money onto the table beside his plate. "Your aunt was my friend, Cleo. In some ways, she was closer to me than my mother, and she was unfailingly generous. If someone needed her help, she gave it without stopping to calculate the cost. So if you want to know whether you'll be getting a bill for services rendered, the answer's no. All I'm trying to do is balance the books."

A noble sentiment, Cleo thought. So why aren't I reassured?

She followed Joe out of the coffee shop and across the parking lot, less disturbed by what he had said than by the things he had left unsaid. Although he had promised he wouldn't send her a bill, nothing he'd told her precluded his demanding some sort of payment.

An errant breeze tugged at the business card in her hand, distracting her, as Joe stopped beside his silver-gray BMW. While he loaded her luggage into the trunk, she traced the engraving on the card with her forefinger, feeling its richness.

Joe had said, "We're in business to make a profit," and the evidence she had seen so far supported the conclusion that his investment in G & G Associates had paid handsome dividends. His take-charge attitude, the way he dressed, the fact that he had stayed in the area's most expensive motel, the quality of his business card; everything about him spoke of prosperity.

He opened the passenger door and helped her into the sedan, and the bucket seat she sank into spoke of prosperity too. The interior of the car even smelled luxurious.

She inhaled deeply, breathing in the odors of leather upholstery and plush wool carpeting: the well-oiled scent of opulence. She heard the hum of the engine, felt the car's smooth acceleration, and asked herself whether a man with Joe's conspicuous liking for the trappings of wealth would invest two months of his time—and heaven knew what other resources—in a project that offered nothing in return.

No way, she thought. Perhaps Joe believed he was doing this out of affection for her great-aunt, but Cleo didn't. Not for a minute.

She had seen the profit motive in operation too many times. She had seen its insidious effect on the people closest to her; seen it change her mother and her grandmother from warm, loving women to spiteful strangers. And if Joe expected a payoff, didn't that imply that Elspeth might have left some sort of treasure after all?

My God! Cleo thought. If she did leave a treasure, my money troubles could be over. I could pay off the loan on the gallery and do some remodeling, maybe even swing a buying trip or two. I could hire a clerk, trade in the station wagon for one of those new minivans . . .

A gust of wind buffeted the car, jarring Cleo from her dreams of financial solvency. She looked about, taking stock of her surroundings just as a spattering of raindrops hit the windshield, leaving splatters as big around as nickels.

"Looks like we're in for it," Joe muttered, assessing the plum-colored clouds ahead. "Damn! I'd hoped we'd make it to the island before the rain started."

"Do you think the ferry will be running?" Cleo asked.

"Can't say," Joe replied. "You know how Wilbur is. Drunk or sober, it's hard to predict what he'll do."

Cleo murmured agreement. For some reason, she wasn't surprised that Wilbur Banks still piloted the ferry from the quaint coastal village of Jarman to Chelsea Island, and to the unnamed peninsula beyond. She smiled, recalling Wilbur's fear of water in any form, but especially of bathing in the stuff—or drinking it.

"Rusts a man's innards," Wilbur claimed. "Saps his strength."

Wilbur's phobia included rain, but even in the mildest weather, when there wasn't a cloud in the sky and the Pacific was living up to its name, he had been known to suspend service. He excused these lapses by saying he had been "indisposed," when everyone knew he had been on another of his benders.

"Maybe this is a local squall," she said. But before she'd finished speaking, the few swollen raindrops became a deluge.

Joe turned the wipers on and slanted a grin her way. "Or maybe we can outrun it." He gunned the motor, and Cleo laughed aloud, exhilarated by a rare sense of freedom, as the car picked up speed. She watched trees and fence posts and road signs whizzing by, and with every mile they traveled she felt more carefree. And then, just north of Manchester Beach, a florist's van slowed their progress.

Cleo stared at the vehicle through the sheeting rain. It wasn't as battered as the van she had seen so often, it was a different color, and it wasn't a Dodge, yet seeing it, she tensed.

The business card cut into her palm, and her gaze darted from the van to the card to Joe's profile, etched against the window.

"The man!" she cried.

Joe stamped on the brake and hunched over the wheel, looking wildly from one side of the highway to the other.

"What man? Where?"

47

"The one who was following me last week."

"Jeez, Cleo! Is that all?" Joe downshifted and eased his foot from the brake to the gas pedal. "I thought we were about to run over someone!"

"I saw him everywhere I went, Joe. He was sallow and heavyset and sort of slimy-looking—"

"And he wore an orange and green aloha shirt," Joe finished.

"Then you *do* know him."

"Yes. He's one of our best operatives."

"If he's your best it's a wonder you have any clients. You ought to tell him to clean up his act. I spotted him almost immediately."

"What counts is that he got the job done," said Joe. "Tell me, did he ever frighten you?"

"No. I was more puzzled by him than alarmed." She grimaced with distaste. "He looked like a scuzzball, but not a sinister scuzzball."

"The defense rests," said Joe. "You see, I was tied up with another case, so I couldn't make it to Mendocino for a few days, and his instructions were to keep you under surveillance, submit daily reports of your activities, and let me know if you made any moves to leave town. But I didn't want to scare you."

"But if he'd been less noticeable, I might never have known he was following me."

"Maybe not." Joe sounded dubious. "I don't like to leave anything to chance though, and besides, I didn't want to embarrass you."

"Embarrass me? How?"

"Like I said, I received daily reports. For all I know you might be a con artist or a mugger. You might cheat at cards or attend orgies six nights out of seven. But as

48

long as you knew you were being watched, you weren't likely to get yourself into any compromising situations."

"Not unless I was an exhibitionist," Cleo replied.

Joe's eyes widened as if he were startled by her comeback. Then he grinned and winked at her, and for the space of a few pulsebeats she was drawn into the tantalizing web of his charm. But before the web could entangle her, she tore her gaze away from his and ducked her head to hide the rush of color to her cheeks.

She wanted to cringe when she thought how boring those daily reports must have been. The most exciting thing she'd done last week was file her income tax returns, and she felt she should apologize to Joe for leading such a bland, uneventful existence.

But wasn't that the way she wanted it?

She'd had an overdose of excitement as a little girl—so much emotional upheaval that when her grandmother's death had left her free to decide her own future, with enough of a nest egg to see her through college and established in a career, her first decision had been, stop the roller coaster, I want to get off.

Since then she had sought stability. She lived quietly, without complications, without excitement, but not without a sense of accomplishment. Her wants were simple; her needs few. She found pleasure in ordinary things: a hard day's work ending in restful sleep, a life at the edge of the sea and one or two close friends to share it, books to read, music to listen to, food to sustain her, and the occasional painting that provided a feast for her eyes. Last spring she had planted petunias in some window boxes; watching them bloom had been a celebration. A walk on the beach gave her a natural high. Seeing a sunset was intoxicating.

49

She had plotted a tranquil course, and this side trip to Chelsea was a detour, nothing more. For the next ten days she would follow Joe down memory lane, and when her visit was over she would return to Mendocino, he would go back to his detective agency in San Francisco, and she would probably never see him again.

So why should she feel self-conscious? Why should she be on guard, holding her breath, wanting Joe to smile at her again? Why should she be waiting for him to make a play for her?

And why had she been cursed with such a vivid imagination?

She only had to look at Joe's mouth and she could see his lips softening to kiss her. She looked at his hands, and she could feel him touching her. She imagined herself in his arms, and she could feel the hard length of his body next to hers and the hot surge of his arousal. . . .

That's *enough,* Cleo told herself. Stop it right there.

Moments ago she had been self-conscious; now her face was burning with embarrassment. She rested her forehead against the coolness of the window, and when she moved away she saw that the glass was steamy. She scrubbed the window clear with the side of her hand, destroying the evidence of the wayward turn her thoughts had taken before Joe could see it.

His business card was crumpled in her other hand, and she tucked it out of sight in her handbag. Taking a deep, steadying breath, she turned to Joe and said, "Now, about my aunt's plans for this house party . . ."

50

CHAPTER FOUR

A mile north of Jarman, Highway 1 plunges along a
windswept bluff in a series of steep, hairpin curves. The
Pacific hugs one side of the road. Rocky cliffs jut up from
the other. The more accessible granite outcroppings are
covered with graffiti; initials mostly, and faded peace
symbols, and political slogans that exhort the passerby to
VOTE NO ON PROPOSITION 13 and FREE NELSON
MANDELA.

Some courageous soul had scaled the face of the cliff to
reach a ledge that seemed suspended in space. There, in
chest-high letters, he had painted JESUS SAVES. Beneath
that doctrine, like the fine print in a contract, another
climber had added THE WHALES.

The rugged terrain left no room for billboards to ad-
vertise the presence of a town, and since Jarman was
barely a speck on the official highway map, it took travelers by surprise. They simply rounded the last switch-
back and there it was.

If motorists happened to be exceeding the speed limit,
and many of them were when they reached the bottom of
the grade, the two-block stretch of Jarman's business district was behind them before they could slow down. At
that point, with no place to turn around, most travelers

went on to Bodega Bay—which was fine with the locals. They were a clannish lot, and although the village derived a good deal of income from speeding tickets, the merchants didn't cater to the tourist trade.

Cleo knew all this, but as Joe guided the BMW along Main Street on that rainy Friday, she was astonished to see how little the town had changed. The grade school had burned down. Hennessey's Dry Goods was getting a much needed face-lift, and Nugent's Café had a new sign, but there were no golden arches, no fitness centers, and not a single automatic teller marred the clock tower outside the savings and loan. Jarman, Cleo thought, must have looked much like this in the twenties, when Aunt Elspeth was my age.

Just beyond the Odd Fellows Hall, Joe made a right turn onto the gravel road that led to the waterfront. They drove past a ships chandlery and crossed the railroad spur that served the sawmill. Between stacks of fresh-milled lumber, Cleo caught a glimpse of the harbormaster's shack.

"The gale warning's up," she said, noticing the pennants at the top of the flagstaff.

"Not much wind here though," Joe observed. "And the rain's stopped. Maybe we're in luck." He pulled off the lane in front of the shack, killed the motor, and stepped out of the car. "Keep your fingers crossed," he said. "I'll see if I can find Wilbur."

He cut across the ragged patch of lawn toward the shack, and just as he disappeared inside, a watery ray of sunlight broke through the clouds. Taking this as a good omen, Cleo climbed out of the sedan and strolled along the beach until she came to the long wooden pier where the ferry docked.

A gull wheeled and cried overhead, then swooped low over the water, providing an escort as she walked to the end of the pier. She counted more than a dozen commercial fishing boats anchored in the harbor. In the distance she could see the humped, sandy hills of the peninsula, but the breakwater prevented her seeing Chelsea Island, which nestled, snug as a cork in a bottle, at the mouth of the bay.

A harsh, guttural noise, not unlike a saw being dragged across metal, drew Cleo's attention to the ferry. She heard the sound again and stepped closer to the boat. A glance through the portholes told her the wheelhouse and passenger cabin were deserted. The tide was out, and she had to brace her hands against a piling and lean over the edge of the pier in order to see the deck.

The noise was repeated a third time. It seemed to come from a bundle of dirty laundry someone had left near the stern. Then the bundle moved, and Cleo realized that what she had mistaken for a pile of grimy clothing was actually a man.

He flopped onto his back and lay there, flaccid as a rag doll, smelling like a distillery, eyes shut, grizzled cheeks sunken, mouth agape. For a minute or more, he didn't move, and then his chest rose as he inhaled and Cleo recognized the sound he was making as a snore.

She was about to return to the harbormaster's shack to tell Joe she had found Wilbur Banks when she spotted him walking toward the pier, a suitcase in each hand.

"No sign of Wilbur," Joe called as he approached.

"He's here." Cleo motioned toward the ferry. "Dead to the world."

Joe propped one foot against the gunnel and bent down to take a look. "Dead drunk is more like it."

53

Wilbur snorted and shifted about, crooking one elbow over his eyes so that Cleo noticed the empty whiskey bottle clutched in his other hand.

"What do we do now?" she asked.

"Sober him up," said Joe. "I'll move the car and get the rest of the luggage while you make a pot of coffee."

It was late afternoon before Wilbur was sober enough to skipper the ferry. By then Joe had begun to worry about the weather and Cleo had begun to fret because her cousins hadn't shown up.

"Do you suppose they got here before we did?" she asked Joe.

"If they did they must've sprouted wings and flown to the island. Wilbur hasn't seen them."

"Wilbur's not the most reliable informant, Joe. He's too busy seeing pink elephants to identify his customers."

"True," Joe allowed, smiling. "But in this case, I believe him. He says the only passengers he's taken to Chelsea this week are the ladies I hired to open the house."

While Wilbur tinkered with the engine, preparing to get under way, Cleo paced the length of the pier, keeping an anxious eye on the road from the village, watching for a car with Ohio license plates. She put off boarding the ferry until the last moment, even though Joe insisted there was no cause for alarm.

"It's a long drive from Ohio to California," he said. "They've probably been detained by car trouble or highway construction."

By the time Wilbur had the ferry's engine idling smoothly, Cleo had to lean into the wind when she walked. Whitecaps scudded over the surface of the bay and a fine drizzle had started to fall. Still, she tried to coax Joe into delaying their departure.

"Can't we wait just a few minutes longer?" she pleaded.

Joe scanned the darkening sky. "It's now or never, Cleo. From the look of those clouds, the storm front's taken a turn toward shore." He offered a hand, helping her aboard, and then cast off the bowline and stern line.

The ferry had scarcely cleared the breakwater before the howling wind struck it with the force of a battering ram.

The engine sputtered, and the deck shuddered beneath Cleo's feet as the ferry struggled to make way against the squall. She heard the whine of the propeller when the boat reached the crest of a wave and hovered there momentarily before skidding into the trough, giving her a sensation of falling into nothingness. Cleo felt the pitch and roll of the vessel as it wallowed free of its watery valley and began its ascent of the next wave, but when Joe suggested she take cover in the passenger cabin, she shook her head.

She clung to a capstan, teeth clenched so tightly her jaws ached, while the rain pelted down on her and the wind tore at her hair and the salt spray stung her cheeks and her mouth filled with the bitterness of nausea. It didn't help that Joe seemed oblivious to the storm. Heedless of danger, he roamed from the engine well to the wheelhouse, tightening cleats and checking the bilge pumps, and when one towering wave washed over the bow, burying him in a wall of water, Cleo bit her lip and thought I will not scream, *I will not scream.*

In fine weather, with calm seas and a fair following wind, the trip from Jarman Harbor to Chelsea Island took less than thirty minutes. That afternoon the trip took an hour—the longest hour of Cleo's life; an hour so frightening, it seemed endless.

In the final fifteen minutes, her thoughts turned toward her father. Her memories of him were fuzzy. He'd been on tour so much, most of what she knew about him was secondhand; tidbits of information garnered from others' recollections of Roger Dennis.

Her grandmother had spoken of him in glowing terms, her mother less favorably. To his fans he'd been an idol; to his fellow musicians, an inspiration; to impresarios, a packed house. But to his daughter, he would always remain a mystery. She had listened to his records, of course, and read the newspaper accounts of his death, and now that she was certain her own life hung in the balance, she found herself wondering what he had done when the *Fair Wind* capsized. Had he reacted bravely? Had he met death with resignation, or had he fought it? Or, like her, had he been immobilized by fear?

Her panic had reached the stage of physical inertia, but her mind was racing, forming prayers for her own safety, for Joe's, for Wilbur's, and when at last Chelsea loomed out of the mist, she understood why Wilbur sought courage in a bottle.

Once the ferry chugged into the lee of the island, the wind abated. For the last mile of the passage, they had smooth sailing, but Cleo did not release her hold on the capstan until the boat had been secured at the dock, next to the *Fair Wind II*. Her fingers felt as if they were bonded to the metal. She had to pry them loose. Her knees gave way when she tried to walk, but Joe was at her side, his arm about her waist to help her disembark.

56

He had to lift her bodily over the stern rail to the landing, where Wilbur Banks waited, whiskey bottle in hand.

"Have a jolt of this," Wilbur invited. "Fix you up, good as new."

Cleo doubted anything could do that, but her lips moved in a silent thank you. She was shivering so badly, the bottle chattered against her teeth. Joe steadied it for her, and she took a long swig.

The whiskey burned her lips and the lining of her nose. It left a raw, medicinal aftertaste, but it eased the paralysis that gripped her, enabling her to repeat her thanks aloud as she returned the bottle to Wilbur.

"My pleasure," he replied.

He took a drink, then passed the bottle to Joe, and for the next quarter hour the two men stood companionably in the shelter of the boathouse, passing the bottle back and forth while they rehashed the afternoon's adventures.

Cleo longed for a hot bath and a change of clothing. The slightest current of air cut through her skirt and sweater, chilling her to the bone. Her hair was plastered to her face and neck in dripping rat tails, her hands were numb, and her nails were turning blue, but she did not object to the delay. Once upon a time, she had dreamed about being marooned on an island with Joe. Now that the dream might become reality, she felt oddly unwilling to be alone with him—especially on Chelsea, where temptation lurked around every corner, waiting to shatter her defenses.

But all too soon the bottle was empty and Wilbur announced it was time he headed home.

"What's the rush?" she said. "Why not come up to the house till the storm passes?"

"No need," Wilbur replied.

"He'll be okay," said Joe. "The wind'll be at his back. He'll be running with the tide."

" 'Sides," Wilbur added, "I'm outta whiskey."

Joe had already begun loading their suitcases onto one of the golf carts, which were the most practical means of conveyance on the island, and when the last piece of luggage had been transferred, he clamped a hand on Wilbur's shoulder and steered him toward the ferry.

"There's the matter of payment," Wilbur reminded him.

"Right," Joe agreed, folding some bills into Wilbur's hand. "And here's a little extra to help you remember our bargain."

Wilbur did a double take when he saw the denomination on the last bill Joe had given him. "Pleasure doin' business with you," he said, pumping Joe's hand.

Joe's mouth was smiling, but his eyes were grim as he waved the older man aboard and cast off for him. He watched the ferry ease away from the dock before he grabbed Cleo's arm and marched her toward the golf cart.

"Why the hell were you so anxious to have Wilbur stay?" he demanded.

"Why were you so anxious to get rid of him?"

"Because of your cousins. Why else? How are they supposed to get over from the mainland if the ferry's not in port?"

Cleo twisted free of Joe's hold and climbed into the cart. "Do you expect me to believe that?"

"Careful, Cleo. That sounded like an accusation."

"What if it is?"

"Then I think you'd better tell me what you're accusing me of."

"I'm not sure what your game is. Not yet. But I saw how much money you gave Wilbur, and I know that fifty dollars is a bit excessive for a tip."

Joe sighed and got behind the wheel. "If you were close enough to see me pay him, you must've heard what the fifty was for."

"Yes," she answered coolly. "I did hear something about a bargain."

"And you naturally assumed I was up to no good."

"And you're naturally going to deny it."

The way Joe's hands knotted around the wheel made Cleo wonder if she had tried his patience too far. His movements were stiff with indignation as he started the engine, and he peeled away from the landing much too quickly. He continued picking up speed until they were hurtling along a rutted trail hardly wide enough to be called a footpath, traveling much too fast for the route he had chosen to take them from the landing to the house.

They forded a shallow stream, plumes of muddy water spurting out behind them. Then the trail forked and they were climbing a hill, winding through the trees, pine boughs slapping against the sides of the cart. Every time they hit a pothole or whipped around a curve, Cleo was obliged to hold on to her seat with both hands to keep from bouncing into the ditch. At the top of the hill, the woods thinned and the trail converged with the main drive to the lodge. She breathed a bit easier, but neither of them spoke again until the cart lurched to a stop near the veranda.

Joe stretched one arm along the back of the seat, draped the other over the wheel, and turned to her, his face taut and expressionless. "Are you interested in the truth, or would you rather think the worst of me?" he asked.

Cleo shook the hair out of her eyes, the better to glare at him, and did not reply.

"You can dish out the truth, but you can't take it," he said. "You'd rather believe a lie than admit you can trust me."

It's myself I don't trust, Cleo thought. If her cousins didn't arrive soon, she was not at all sure that she would be able to keep her distance from Joe. Her gaze shied away from his. She started to step out of the cart, but Joe's hand fastened on her arm, pinning her to the seat.

"Let me go," she cried.

"Not a chance, Cleo. You're not going anywhere till you've heard me out."

She tried to pull away, but his grip tightened. After a brief, uneven struggle, his arms closed around her, capturing her in a punishing embrace. But his touch was bliss. His hands played over her, tracing the fine-boned wings of her shoulder blades and coasting along her rib cage to the slope of her hips. He measured the span of her waist, outspread fingers pressing into her flesh, fitting her softness to him, and a shock of awareness shot through her.

If she tipped her head ever so slightly, their lips would meet.

In a feeble attempt to overcome the urge to kiss him, she closed her eyes, but the instant her eyelids drifted shut, she felt surrounded by Joe, consumed by him. She felt herself melting against his hardness, dissolving in his warmth. Her body had gone slack and yielding, and her heart was pounding, pounding . . .

"I'll listen," she conceded. "Only let me go."

60

Joe exhaled on a sigh and slowly, almost reluctantly, released her. It gave Cleo no satisfaction that his breathing was as labored as her own.

"Tell me about the fifty dollars," she prompted.

"It's a down payment. Wilbur gets another fifty when the house party's over."

"Even with inflation, a hundred dollars ought to cover a whole lot of boat rides, Joe. How many fares are you paying?"

"Just yours, mine, and your cousins', but the hundred's a bonus. I guess you could say it's a tip, although I look on it as an insurance policy."

"What are you insuring?"

"Wilbur's silence. He's agreed to give us pickup-and-delivery service, rain or shine, and he won't tell a soul what's going on out here."

"You realize, don't you, that you might have defeated your purpose. With fifty dollars, Wilbur could buy enough booze to stay drunk for a week."

"Sure he could, but he won't. He gave me his word."

"And you expect him to keep it?"

Joe shrugged and got out of the cart. "You've gotta trust someone, Cleo."

"Not a man whose price is a hundred dollars," she replied. Silently, she added, And not you either, Joe Gamble.

The storm intensified while Cleo was in the tub. The water was only tepid, so instead of lingering in her bath, she settled for a brisk rubdown with a towel.

Her bedroom was chilly and full of shadows, even with the lamps lighted. The rain drummed against the roof, the gale rattled the windowpanes, and above the keening

61

wind she could hear the distant thunder of the surf. But an unnatural silence radiated from the floor register. The metal grating was clammy to the touch. Joe had promised he'd have the furnace going in no time, but evidently he had encountered some difficulty.

She dried her hair as well as she could and dressed in her warmest slacks, a bulky knit sweater, and woolly knee socks. She didn't bother with shoes. She was shivering, but not entirely from the cold, as she went in search of Joe.

She hurried along the corridor, past empty, echoing rooms, not stopping till she reached the top of the stairs. There she paused to survey the massive proportions of the foyer, which soared two stories from parquet floor to paneled ceiling.

No gloom here, she thought, admiring the Waterford chandelier. Its ornate brass chain vanished in the darkness overhead, but the chandelier itself was brilliant as diamonds and so fragile it seemed to float in midair. It dominated the entryway, dazzled the eye, and spilled light into the most remote corners of the room.

She ran her hand over the banister, the same lustrous walnut as the ceiling, and recalled the times she had ridden it to the first floor. Like sledding without the sled, she thought. Her lips curved into a smile as she recalled the sensation of speed, the thrill of defying her grandmother's rules of ladylike decorum.

Do I dare? Cleo wondered.

She touched the balustrade with one finger, testing its smoothness, and after a cautious look around the foyer assured her that Joe was nowhere in sight, she sat astride the banister.

"Here goes nothing," she murmured.

She counted down from ten and pushed off, and then she was sliding, zooming past the family portraits that lined the staircase, gathering momentum until she felt as if she were flying. She spun around the curve in the banister and her heart jumped into her throat. Her stomach hadn't caught up with her yet, and it was scary and exciting and *fun!* She felt the warm buildup of friction through the seat of her slacks, heard the chimes from the cut-crystal teardrops in the chandelier as she rushed past, and laughed aloud with the sheer joy of reliving this childhood prank.

Just before she reached the foot of the stairs she glanced over her shoulder, gauging the distance to the bottom. She caught a hint of movement from the corner of her eye and realized Joe had wandered into the foyer. His presence made her forget the trick of braking herself to a stop before she ran out of banister.

She catapulted over the end of the railing and would have made a painful one-point landing if Joe hadn't broken her fall. She hit him, rump first, in the solar plexus. He doubled over with the force of the impact and his arms hooked around her. The crown of her head bumped his chin, jarring his teeth together. The blow knocked him off balance, and he staggered backward four or five steps. Through some miracle, he maintained both his grip on her and his footing. All he lost was his cool.

He barked an oath as he set her on her feet, and the instant her toes touched the floor, she stammered an apology.

"Are you all right?" she inquired, stricken.

"I think so," Joe answered dazedly, rubbing his jaw. He thrust his chin from side to side and opened his mouth as wide as he could, closing it with a snap. Concluding everything was in working order, he gave her a lopsided grin. "Did you get the license number of the truck?"

Cleo managed a sheepish smile. "I guess I must've looked pretty ridiculous, huh?"

Joe's gaze roved over her, taking in her flushed cheeks, the sparkle in her eyes, the hectic·rise and fall of her breasts beneath the teal green sweater.

"I'd say sliding down banisters agrees with you. You should do it more often."

"Once was enough," Cleo said. "Grandmother Dennis must be spinning in her grave."

"But Elspeth would be delighted. So would your great-grandpa."

"I suspect that's true. I can imagine good old Crazy sliding down the banister himself. But how about the rest of the Jarmans?"

Following the direction of Cleo's glance, Joe studied the gilt-framed portraits that ascended the wall above the staircase. The paintings were relentlessly somber: bearded patriarchs wearing stiff black coats, high starched collars, and stern expressions.

"Gentlemen all," he said dryly.

"Prudes to the core," said Cleo.

"Where are their womenfolk?"

"They probably took one look at the way their husbands' pictures turned out and refused to sit for the artist."

Joe nodded. "These men were Elspeth's uncles and great-uncles," said Joe.

"Which might explain why she took off for New York the day she turned eighteen," Cleo joked.

Joe chuckled and waved one hand toward the por-

64

traits. "Tell me, Cleo, do you feel any affection for these men?"

"Heavens, no! As far as I'm concerned, they're just a collection of bad paintings."

"Then why should you care if they would approve of you?"

Cleo cleared her throat. "I don't," she said. On the surface her denial seemed adamant, but Joe noticed her hesitation, the quick clearing of her throat.

She does care, he thought. Why won't she admit it?

Before he could ask, Cleo changed the subject. "Listen to that wind," she said. "I think it's gotten worse."

"It has," he agreed. "It's turned into a real nor'wester."

She crossed to the window and looked out. "Do you suppose my cousins will decide to stay in town till the storm blows over?"

"Yes, I do. I talked to Wilbur on the CB while you were upstairs. He says they were waiting at the wharf when he got back to town. I expect they'll be here some-time tomorrow."

"Well, that's a relief," said Cleo.

She didn't sound relieved—didn't look it either. She looked pale, worried, jumpy. The strong overhead light emphasized the mauve smudges beneath her eyes. The corners of her mouth drooped with weariness, yet she held herself rigidly in check.

She started when Joe linked arms with her, and he smiled, hoping to put her at ease. "I've built a fire in the parlor," he said. "Why don't we go in there? I don't know about you, but I could use a drink."

She stared at him as if he'd suggested she eat a bug, but she offered no resistance as he ushered her along the broad central hallway. Maybe she was tired of bickering. God knew he was. It had been a long, trying day, not an auspicious beginning for the house party. His feet felt like blocks of ice, and he'd be lucky if he didn't catch pneumonia, running around in wet clothes. Wilbur's rotgut had given him a headache, he'd skinned his knuckles trying to get the furnace going, and to top it all off, he was starving.

He didn't know which he wanted most: a hot shower, supper, or bed. But one thing was certain. He didn't want to fight with Cleo anymore. Not tonight.

So we're alone, Cleo thought. No one else in the house, on the island . . .

Her legs had a strange hollow feeling, as if they belonged to someone else. It's just for tonight, she told herself. We're adults. There's no need to panic.

Joe opened the wide double doors to the parlor and a wave of warmth greeted them.

Applewood logs burned on the hearth, spicing the air with their fragrance. In front of the fireplace, at either end of a wine velvet love seat, table lamps with pink fringed shades created a rosy pool of light. Like the foyer, the parlor was huge; more than twice the size of Cleo's bedroom, and much more cluttered. Knickknacks covered every available surface, without regard for logic or aesthetics. A glass-domed bouquet of wax flowers jockeyed for position with Remington's Pony Express rider, who jostled a bisque shepherdess, who rubbed shoulders with a miniature Venus de Milo. There were seashells and paperweights and ashtrays that said SOUVENIR OF NIAGARA FALLS. Antimacassars blossomed on chair arms and

66

sofa backs, peacock feathers sprouted in one corner of the room, a Boston fern grew in another.

And who knows what else? Cleo thought.

Now and again Elspeth Jarman had gone through the motions of sorting out the personal effects her relatives had amassed, but each memento reminded her of a person, a place, an incident, a precise moment in time. She would rearrange things, occasionally she would consign some trinket to the attic, but she never, *never* threw anything away.

The parlor had been Elspeth's favorite room in the house. On afternoons when inclement weather kept her indoors, she had written her poetry seated by the bay windows, which offered a view of the sunset. In the evening she had held court by the fireside. The stamp of her personality was strongest here, almost tangible. As Cleo picked her way through the clutter to the fireplace, she thought she caught a whiff of her aunt's perfume, elusive jasmine mingling with aromatic applewood.

"What can I get you?" Joe called from the shadows behind the bar.

"Southern Comfort if you have it, scotch if you—no, wait. What was that sherry Aunt Elspeth used to drink?"

"Amontillado."

"That's what I'll have," said Cleo.

Joe smiled. "Seems fitting."

While he poured their drinks, she looked through the photographs on the mantel for the picture of Elspeth in her Follies costume. At fourteen, looking at that photo, Cleo had not been impressed. She hadn't seen beyond her aunt's beaded dress, Cupid's bow lips, and rouged knees. Now, however, she recognized Elspeth's vitality, her earthy appeal.

"Quite the bombshell, wasn't she?" Joe handed Cleo a ruby-banded cordial glass and sat on the love seat, his legs extended toward the fire.

"Yes, she was."

"Place doesn't seem the same without her."

Joe's voice sounded thick, and a lump of tears gathered in Cleo's throat, partly from empathy, partly regret.

"I wish I'd known her better," she murmured.

"You'll have your chance the next ten days. That's what this house party's all about."

Cleo returned Elspeth's photograph to its spot on the mantel and took a sip of sherry. "I wanted to thank you for putting me in my old room."

"My mother's idea," said Joe. "She thought you'd like it."

"Oh. Well, then would you thank her for me?" Cleo watched the flames leaping on the hearth and wondered why she felt disappointed. "How is your mother?"

"Same as ever, only more so. She's managing a sorority house in San Diego. I've tried to talk her into retiring, but she won't hear of it."

"Chelsea doesn't seem the same without her," said Cleo.

"I'll tell her you said that. She'll be pleased." Joe drank the last of his sherry, got to his feet, and stretched. "I think I'll have a shower," he said. He strode toward the hall and Cleo hurried after him, reluctant to be alone.

"Did you have any luck with the furnace?" she asked.

"Not much, but I got the water heater working."

"How about the kitchen?"

"Everything's A-OK in there. The ladies who opened the house helped me make out a shopping list, so the

68

freezer's stocked and there's all kinds of stuff in the cupboards."

"Then maybe I'll start dinner. Is there anything special you'd like?"

"Just lots of whatever you fix." Joe was halfway up the stairs before it dawned on him that Cleo was stalling. He turned to look at her and saw her apprehension. "I won't be long," he said. "If you need anything in the meantime, all you have to do is knock at my door."

"Which room are you in?"

"I'm just across the hall from you."

Joe continued up the stairs, whistling under his breath, and Cleo stared after him, envying his nonchalance.

Just across the hall, he'd said.

Obviously, he was trying to reassure her, but his effort had backfired. She had never felt less confident in her life.

CHAPTER FIVE

After the cozy disorder of the parlor, the kitchen had the institutional warmth of an operating room. It was unexpectedly modern: stainless steel appliances, white enameled cabinets, white walls, black and white checkered linoleum on the floor. Everything polished and spotless beneath harsh fluorescent lights. Its layout was convenient; as efficient as Joe's mother, who had planned its renovation.

Funny to think of a woman like Mrs. Gamble having a harum-scarum son like Joe. She had come to Chelsea when Joe was an infant, which meant she had worked for Elspeth Jarman almost thirty years, yet so far as Cleo knew, the two women had never called one another by their first names. Since her aunt had been the type who called everybody darling, Cleo assumed it was Joe's mother who had preferred formality. Certainly this seemed consistent with her impression of Mrs. Gamble as unapproachable, unsmiling, dedicated to the proposition that life is a serious business and the future belongs to the solemn.

As Cleo inventoried the supply of groceries in the cupboards, she decided that Joe's mother was the most formidable woman she had ever met; even more dignified than Grandmother Dennis.

While she scrubbed potatoes for baking, Cleo wondered if Mrs. Gamble had a first name. While she tossed the salad, she wondered if there had ever been a Mr. Gamble. Just as she was removing the steaks from the broiler, the power went off, and after that, she was too busy searching for candles to waste time speculating about Joe's mother.

She foraged through drawer after drawer, feeling her way in the darkness. She found a box of squat white candles for a chafing dish, but she couldn't find matches. She was about to resume the search when a narrow beam of light appeared from the dining room.

"Cleo? You in there?" Joe inquired, sweeping the kitchen with his penlight.

"Over here by the pantry. Have you got a match?"

He trained the light on her, and she held up the box of candles. "Sure do," he replied.

"Thank God. I was afraid I'd have to rub some sticks together to light these things."

"Just call me Eveready." Joe lit one of the candles and dropped melted wax onto a saucer, providing a makeshift holder. "How're you doing with supper?"

"Everything's ready."

"And it smells great. Why don't we take it to the parlor?"

He helped her load their dinner onto a tray, along with plates and flatware, a luncheon cloth, and napkins, then clamped the penlight between his teeth and led the way to the parlor, where they spread the food in front of the fire.

Like a picnic, Cleo thought. Only more romantic . . .

"Forgot something," said Joe.

He made a second trip to the kitchen and returned with a bottle of Beaujolais and two stemmed goblets in one hand, a candelabra from the dining table in the other, and a bottle of ketchup tucked beneath his arm, which only slightly marred the ambiance.

Cleo watched him dunk a bite of steak in the ketchup and barely suppressed a shudder. "You're wasting a prime filet," she said.

"Not so. I'm going to eat every bite."

"But you can't taste it. Not with all that goop on it."

"Yes, I can, and it's delicious. So's the salad. Where'd you learn to cook like this?"

Cleo shrugged. "There's nothing complicated about meat and potatoes. All you have to do is bake and broil. One of the men my mother dated was a chef. He taught me some of the basics."

Joe's eyes narrowed. "You know, Cleo, that's the first you've mentioned your mother."

Cleo bent her head. Her hair curtained her face, concealing her from Joe's scrutiny. "Is there some significance in that?"

"Could be. Elspeth used to think you blamed yourself for your mother's death."

"Why would I blame myself?"

"Maybe because you stayed here when Suzanne went to L.A. If you'd gone with her, she might've been with you instead of in that supper club when it caught fire."

Joe refilled their wineglasses, and Cleo kept her head down, avoiding his eyes. She sensed his gaze upon her, intent and probing, as he said, "Elspeth was convinced you were punishing yourself for being alive while Suzanne was dead. She thought that was why you never came back to Chelsea, why you were so hostile to me."

Cleo took a deep breath and let it out slowly. "That's an interesting theory, Joe."

"Is it accurate?"

"I don't know. I try not to think about my mother. If I think about her, I get all mixed up. I get sad and angry and resentful, and then I do feel guilty, and . . . Look, could we drop this?"

"We can if you want to. I just thought, if we resolved this, we might be able to get along with each other. We had some good times, Cleo, in the old days."

"Yes, we did," she agreed.

Joe brushed the silky spill of hair away from her cheek. "Do you remember helping me paint the *Fair Wind*?"

"Helping you?" Cleo stared at him in stunned disbelief. "As I recall you pulled a Tom Sawyer and sat on your duff while I did all the work."

"But it was fun, wasn't it? Besides, you got more paint on yourself and the brightwork than you did on the hull. I had to put in overtime cleaning up after you." Joe chuckled and shook his head. "Or how about the time I taught you to dance?"

"*You* taught *me*?"

"Don't you remember? I gave you I don't know how many lessons right here in this room."

"I'm afraid you're suffering from selective amnesia, Joe. You seem to have forgotten that I knew how to dance long before I met you. When I was only ten I was the star pupil at Madame Robideau's School of the Dance, and at twelve I graduated with honors."

"What did you learn there? The minuet?"

"As a matter of fact, Madame started her classes with

73

the minuet, but she also taught us the foxtrot and the waltz and the cha-cha—as you jolly well know, because I taught them to you."

Joe responded to her irate defense of Madame Robideau with a smile. "What we have here," he said, "is a communications gap."

"How do you mean?"

"Well, for me the word *dancing* is synonymous with the kind of music that makes you want to move your whole body, not just your feet. Dancing should be both a sensual and a spiritual experience. It should be exciting, uninhibited, expressive—"

"And you don't consider the waltz expressive?"

"On a scale of one to ten, I'd give it a three point five."

Cleo placed her knife and fork across her plate carefully, ignoring the urge to hurl them at Joe. Her voice was frosty with disdain as she said, "If you had the capacity to appreciate subtlety, you would recognize that the waltz is lovely and free and eloquent. It's much more expressive than hopping about and shaking your booty and trampling all over your partner's feet."

"Perhaps," Joe allowed dryly. "Then again, it's possible that if my partner had been better coordinated, her feet wouldn't have gotten trampled."

"Are you saying I'm clumsy?" Cleo threw down her napkin. "Listen, fella, I'll have you know I can out-dance you any day of the week."

"Prove it," said Joe, getting to his feet.

"P-pardon me?"

"I said prove it."

"You mean dance? Here? Now?"

"Of course now."

"But there's no music."

74

"Yes, there is. There's your aunt's old Victrola."

With a smug grin, Joe scooped up his penlight and walked to the far corner of the room, where he opened a cabinet and rummaged through Elspeth's record collection.

"Here's one," he said. " 'Three O'clock in the Morning.' "

He cranked the gramophone, put the record on the turntable, and the opening notes of the waltz emanated from the big brass trumpet, distant and scratchy, a bit off key, but definitely music.

He returned for Cleo, self-assurance in every stride. "Okay, Twinkletoes," he said, hauling her up beside him. "Time to put up or shut up."

His arms went around her and she wedged one palm against his shoulder and placed her other hand in his. She held herself stiffly, keeping him at arm's length as he dragged her through an awkward series of steps.

"You're leading," he said.

"Somebody has to," she replied.

He laughed and gave her a gentle shake. His hand cupped the nape of her neck, his fingers rotating in a gentle massage, easing the knots of tension along her spine. "Relax, Cleo. I won't bite. Come closer."

"Not while you're wearing shoes."

The beam of his penlight revealed her stocking feet, and he let her go while he removed his loafers.

"You've got a hole in your sock," she said.

"Picky, picky," he muttered.

"Merely an observation. I'm relieved to see you're not perfect."

The wavering candlelight shadowed his features. She couldn't see his face. But intuition told her he was surprised. He tossed the penlight aside and held out his arms.

"Shall we try again?"

He issued the invitation in a husky drawl that resonated along her nerve ends and sent her pulse rate soaring. When he used that tone she wanted to move her whole body, not just her feet. She wanted to arch her back and rub herself against him like a cat.

Sensual, she thought. *His voice is sensual.*

His touch was sensual too; uninhibited, eloquent, and—

Incendiary.

She felt the hot imprint of his hands, one at her shoulder, the other at her waist, fingers slipping beneath her heavy wool sweater to caress soft bare skin. Exploring, fondling, never still; searching restlessly, in cadence with the waltz. Stroking along her sides now, numbering her ribs, kindling a delicious anticipation as they inched upward to her breasts.

She swayed closer to him, twined her arms about him, pressed her face into the hollow of his shoulder. She felt the scrape of his beard as his lips skimmed her cheek, seeking her lips, and a wild urgency possessed her.

She turned her face toward his and he kissed her, lightly at first, teasing, sampling, then deeply and hungrily. She responded wantonly, welcoming the sweet darting thrusts of his tongue, tasting him, provoking him.

How many times had she dreamed Joe was holding her this way, kissing her this way? As if he never wanted to stop, as if she were the only woman in the world for him.

But his kiss was more exciting than she had imagined; her passion more intense.

The music slowed and their bodies moved in langorous

synchrony around the dark perimeter of the parlor. Glide, two, three; turn, two, three. Knees brushing, thighs touching.

Was that her heart racing, or his?

Then the music stopped, and Joe whispered her name. "Thank you, Cleo," he said.

"For what?"

"Showing me what I've been missing. You're a heck of a dancer. I never knew waltzing could be so much fun."

She took a shaky step away from him. "Nice try, Joe. On a scale of one to ten, I'd give that line a four point five."

"It was supposed to be a compliment."

"And I might be flattered if you meant it."

"What makes you think I don't?"

"It sounded generic. I'll bet you've used it a dozen times before, on a dozen different women."

"Maybe I lack originality, but that doesn't mean I'm insincere." Joe grinned and winked at her. The timbre of his voice deepened as he said, "I'll do better next time, Cleo."

Hours later, Cleo was still seething. His careless assumption that there would be a next time grated. In the privacy of her room, exhausted but too keyed up to sleep, she tossed and turned and punched her pillow, pretending it was Joe, and tried to figure out why the kiss that left her devastated had been only a diversion to him.

Fun he'd called it, as if they were kids playing spin the bottle. But what irritated her most was the realization that Joe had come within a hairsbreadth of seducing her. If the Victrola hadn't wound down, if Joe had held her a few minutes longer, kissed her again, she'd have done anything he suggested. Instead of spending the night alone, she'd probably be across the hall in his bed.

Face it, she told herself. You wanted to make love with him.

She gave the pillow another fierce punch as she admitted that she'd been willing—God, but she'd been willing! She'd practically thrown herself at him, which meant she couldn't trust herself any more than she trusted Joe. The only bright spot in Cleo's long, sleepless night was the recollection that, with her cousins' arrival, she could blend into the crowd.

"There's safety in numbers," she murmured. And she hugged the pillow to her chest, wondering why she found no consolation in this thought.

CHAPTER SIX

The power was on the next morning. Cleo was waiting for the coffee to brew, feeling groggy and heavy-eyed, when a call came over the CB from Wilbur.

"Your cousins are aboard," he said. "We're just leaving the harbor. We'll be docking at Chelsea in thirty minutes."

"Meet you at the landing," she replied.

Joe was still sleeping, but he had left the keys to the golf cart on a pegboard by the back door. She filled a thermos with coffee, pulled a hooded sweatshirt over her blue velour jogging pants, and drove the cart down the main road to the landing. This route took a few minutes longer than the shortcut Joe had chosen, but it was easier going, and she reached the dock with time to spare.

The morning was brisk and breezy, with only a few wispy clouds to mar the fresh-scrubbed blue of the sky. She poured a cup of coffee and drank it sitting at the end of the pier, her back against a piling, her feet dangling over the water.

The thermos was empty and she had begun to feel more curious than sleepy when the ferry steamed into view. She got to her feet and scanned the passengers crowded along the starboard rail. From Joe's descriptions, she began attaching faces to the names of the Ohio Jarmans.

The tiny white-haired lady must be Belle Jarman. "A spinster," Joe had said. "She's in her seventies, but don't let her age fool you. She's got more stamina than most twenty-year-olds."

The stocky, bespectacled man next to Belle would be Andrew Jarman, and the girl next to him must be his daughter Tiffany. According to Joe, Tiffany was a college freshman in open rebellion against her parents, which undoubtedly explained her father's harried look.

"Tiffany dresses early Madonna," Joe had said. "Or maybe it's late Cyndi Lauper. Whatever it is, it's funky. Lace bows in her hair, earrings the size of hubcaps, necklaces big as bedposts. And she puts on makeup with a trowel. If she were my daughter, I wouldn't let her leave the house till she washed her face."

Last but not least of her cousins was Peter Jarman, Tiffany's thirteen-year-old brother. "Watch out for Pete," Joe had cautioned. "I spent two nights at Andy's place, and in that time the little monster short-sheeted my bed, tied knots in my socks, and canceled the reservations for my return flight."

Looking at his offspring, Cleo felt a twinge of sympathy for Andrew Jarman. Tiffany was togged in stovepipe stirrup pants and an oversize scarlet and lavender op-art sweatshirt that hobbled her knees and made her look like a grape. Her hair was spray-painted Day-Glo pink to clash with everything. Peter wore jeans, an Ocean Pacific T-shirt, and Reeboks. He had a Walkman at his hip, a Polaroid camera around his neck, and he could be taken for a typical teenage boy until one spotted his fiendish smirk. Then he seemed slightly less threatening than Attila the Hun.

Cleo wondered what had happened to Andrew's wife. Had Lucille decided to stay in Sandusky? If I were Lucille, I would have, she thought.

As the ferry eased alongside the dock, she waved, but only Belle waved back. Andrew was busy reprimanding his son, and Tiffany had her hands full protecting her hair-spikes from the capricious ocean breezes. Wilbur tossed the bowline and Cleo made it fast while he secured the stern line. Then the boarding ramp was lowered and her cousins were disembarking, and she introduced herself to each of them in turn.

Their responses ran the gamut from affection to rudeness. Belle kissed her on the cheek and chirped, "Well, now, this is a treat," and Peter leered at her through the camera's viewfinder.

"Say cheese," he ordered, and snapped her picture.

Tiffany leaned on her father's arm as she descended the ramp. When Cleo said, "Welcome to Chelsea," the younger woman gave her a blank, uninterested stare and declared, "I'm going to lose my breakfast."

She hurried toward the end of the dock with Peter dogging her heels, Polaroid cocked and at the ready.

Cleo smiled weakly at Andrew, who was shaking her hand. "Is Tiffany all right?"

"She's fine," he answered with false heartiness. "Just a little seasick."

"Tiffany suffers from nervous indigestion," said Belle.

Andrew scowled at his son, who was recording Tiffany's battle with nausea for posterity. "Give your sister a break," he pleaded. "That's enough pictures for a while."

Peter paid no attention to his father's request, and Tiffany muttered, "Little snot."

"Lucille's not with you?" said Cleo.

"No," Belle replied. "She sends her regards, and she asked me to tell you she's looking forward to meeting you some other time, but since Elspeth wasn't a blood relative, she didn't think it would be proper for her to come along." Squaring her shoulders, Belle added, "Why don't you help Mr. Banks with the luggage, Andrew. I'll look after Tiffany."

Despite Belle's efforts to impose order, the scene on the landing quickly became chaotic. Pete seemed to be everywhere at once, exclaiming, "Wow! Scope it out!" and taking pictures of the boathouse and the *Fair Wind II,* the pine-studded bluffs to the north of the dock and the sand dunes to the south. Wilbur was tinkering with the ferry's engine, Tiffany was repairing her makeup, and Belle was acting like a traffic cop, which left only Andrew and Cleo to unload the suitcases. But eventually they stacked a small mountain of luggage next to the golf cart.

"This may take two trips," Cleo announced. "The cart won't hold more than a couple of us."

"Andrew wanted to bring his car," said Belle.

"Damn right I did." Andrew ran a hand through his thinning hair and kicked the cart's rear tire. "It's a Continental. Less than ten thousand miles on the odometer. I bought it expressly for this trip, and I don't like leaving it in a public parking lot."

"I'll keep an eye on it," Wilbur offered. "It'll be safer in town than here."

Andrew looked to Cleo for confirmation. "Is it true there aren't any roads on this island?"

"Well, strictly speaking there are, but they haven't

been maintained in years. They're rough and over-grown—"

"In other words, you agree with Wilbur."

Cleo nodded.

Andrew sighed and gave the tire another kick. "I guess that settles it. All we have to decide now is who gets to make the first trip to the lodge."

"There's also the matter of payment," said Wilbur.

Andrew reached for his wallet, but Cleo stopped him. "That's not necessary," she said. "Mr. Banks has been amply compensated."

"For the ferry service," Wilbur allowed. "Not for baby-sittin' Mr. Jarman's brand new Lincoln."

"I think I'd better tip him," said Andrew.

While he negotiated with Wilbur, Belle and Tiffany debated whether a passenger could ride with the suitcases that were strapped to the back of the golf cart, and Peter took advantage of their distraction by jumping into the cart and driving off. A collective groan rose from his family as he sped across the dunes.

"Do something, Andrew," Belle instructed. "He's liable to hurt himself with that thing."

"Yes, of course." Cupping his hands to his mouth, Andrew bellowed, "Listen up, Peter Jarman. If you know what's good for you, you'll turn that cart around and hightail it back here right now!" Seconds later, the cart disappeared into the pines. So much for a father's stern warning.

"That does it," Tiffany muttered darkly, glaring after her brother. "I could shrivel up and die when I think I gave up spring break in Fort Lauderdale to come to this dumb house party."

"Now, now, kitten. It's only for nine days." Andrew

spoke in a soothing tone, obviously attempting to placate his daughter, but judging by the pout that tugged at Tiffany's lower lip, she wasn't comforted.

Neither was Cleo. In that moment, nine days seemed like an eternity.

At twelve thirty that day, the party assembled for lunch on the veranda, and Peter asked the question that was foremost in everyone's mind.

"When do we start the treasure hunt?"

Joe filled his plate with taco salad before he replied, "The formal kickoff's this evening."

Pete's face fell. "Why do we have to wait till then?"

"Those are the rules, buddy. Besides, Elspeth's clues aren't going to make much sense till you're acquainted with the island, so the first thing on the agenda is a guided tour."

"Do you know what the clues are?" Andrew inquired.

Joe shook his head. "I'm as much in the dark as you are, but if Elspeth was running true to form, they're bound to be tricky."

"And in rhyme," said Belle. Glancing around the table, she explained, "Cousin Elspeth wrote poetry. I have one of her books at home."

"Which one?" asked Cleo.

"I don't rightly recall, dear. It's been ages since I read it, but it seems to me it has a very long title."

Joe exchanged a grin with Cleo and said, "It's gotta be *Things Mama Never Told Me—Or Maybe Not. Perhaps She Did and I Forgot.*"

A wave of laughter swept the table. Even Tiffany looked amused, and Cleo murmured, "I always thought the title was the best thing about that book."

"It's coming back to me now," Belle mused. "I remember a section about love, and one stanza began, 'Love is like champagne punch. When it gets old, it goes flat.'" She smiled and added, "That doesn't rhyme, but in my limited experience, there's an element of truth in it. It's also funny."

"It wasn't meant to be," said Cleo. "Most of Aunt Elspeth's poems were supposed to be profound. She'd write something like, 'All the leaves were dying; barren branches sway. The sky was gray and dismal, but our hearts were young and gay.' And she'd compound her mistake by taking it seriously."

Andrew looked at Cleo over the tops of his glasses, then settled them more squarely on the bridge of his nose. "If that's the best she could do, how did she manage to get her poems published?"

"Vanity press," said Joe. "She paid for the printing, binding, distribution, and promotion."

"Sounds expensive," said Andrew.

"It was," Joe replied. "Especially the advertising. And when you multiply the expenses times three—"

"You mean she actually published more than one book?"

"That's right."

Andrew was punching figures into his pocket calculator, estimating the costs. He pressed the equal key and stared at the total, dumbstruck. Belle read the display of numbers over his shoulder and said, "I gather this publishing venture is an example of the bad investments you told us about."

"One of them, yes." Joe studied the appleblossom design on the rim of his plate as if it were a balance sheet as he went on. "You have to understand, Elspeth inherited her father's eccentricities, but not his shrewdness. She was a soft touch for anyone with a hard luck story, and she had a weakness for show business. She backed several musical comedies, and they all closed out of town. Then, through Suzanne, she got interested in movie production. She financed a number of projects to further Suzanne's acting career. They showed a profit, but she plowed the whole bundle into *Rivals,* which turned out to be a major flop."

"Let me get this straight," said Andrew. "Are you telling us Elspeth died broke?"

"I'm saying it's possible." Joe frowned and chased an olive around his plate with his fork. "On the other hand, old Samuel Jarman had the Midas touch. He pioneered lumbering and fishing along this stretch of the coast, and in the process he accumulated a fortune. He also developed a reputation for being a maverick."

Belle nodded sagely. "I remember my papa saying his uncle Samuel delighted in shocking people and doing the unexpected."

Tiffany stirred sugar into her iced tea and tried to look bored. "According to Mr. Banks, everyone called Samuel 'Crazy' Jarman."

"That's right," Joe replied. "The way I heard the story, one of the carpenters who worked on the lodge made the comment that a man would have to be crazy to build on the island when he owned fine tracts of acreage on the mainland. That's how the nickname got started, and because Samuel was eccentric, it stuck, but Elspeth claimed no one ever called her father Crazy to his face. The townspeople depended on him for their livelihood, and they weren't about to alienate the goose that laid the golden egg."

Which bring us full circle, thought Cleo. Back to the treasure hunt, and to the unresolved question of whether there truly is a treasure. This time no one put the question into words. Even Pete remained silent.

She glanced at Andrew and Belle, trying to decipher their expressions, looking for traces of avarice beneath their bland surface politeness. All she saw was that Andrew was perspiring in the midday heat and Belle was getting sunburned. Her forehead was pink and her nose was peeling. Combined with her prominent teeth and sprightly manner, her heightened color made her resemble a rabbit.

But there was nothing rabbitlike about Tiffany. She was sipping her drink and practicing her predatory wiles on Joe, flirting with him behind her long lashes. She wasn't terribly skilled. In fact, she was quite blatant, but Joe pretended he didn't notice. He shifted about, edging closer to Cleo.

As the silence lengthened, Pete heaved an elaborate sigh and began fidgeting with his camera.

Obviously, he was getting restless, and so was Cleo. She became aware of Joe's forearm nudging hers, and her heart skipped a beat. She was tempted to return the pressure, but too much nudging could be dangerous. It might be habit forming.

They had a lot of ground to cover, most of it over rough terrain, so Joe drew a map for Belle, marking the easiest routes and points of interest, and after agreeing to rendezvous at the abandoned Coast Guard station near the northwest end of the island, she left in one of the golf carts.

A few minutes later the rest of the party set off on the trail that bisected the rocky spine of the island, with Peter racing ahead, Tiffany bringing up the rear, and Joe, Andrew, and Cleo trooping along between them. Andrew was red-faced and winded before they'd hiked a quarter mile.

"This is what I get for being a CPA," he said. "Out of shape."

Joe vaulted over a fallen pine that blocked the path, then reached back to pull the older man over the obstacle. "We can stop for a breather if you want."

"I'll go the distance," Andrew panted. "But it occurs to me that Elspeth couldn't have made this excursion, even in a golf cart."

"No, she couldn't."

"Then why are we?"

"Two reasons," said Joe. "Elspeth wanted you to see all of Chelsea, and she had help planting her clues."

Andrew lengthened his stride, trying to keep up with the pace Joe had set. "What sort of help?" he asked.

"The senior class at Jarman High," Joe replied. "She invited the students over for a barbecue last fall, and while they were here, she gave each of them something to hide for her."

"I see," said Andrew. "How large is this class?"

"Forty, maybe fifty students. But there are less than a dozen clues."

"So most of them hid blinds?"

Joe glanced over his shoulder, keeping track of Tiffany, who was lagging some distance behind. "In a way, all of them did."

"How so?"

"The kids had no idea what they were hiding. Elspeth made up her packets in quintuplicate, one real, four dummies. The kids thought she was being weird."

"Did one of the students hide the treasure?"

"No, that honor went to the president of the county chapter of the Native Sons."

"Is he a man of integrity?"

"I've never heard otherwise. Anyway, Elspeth filed an inventory with her attorney and this guy knew it."

"What about the students?" asked Cleo. "How can we be sure they followed Aunt Elspeth's instructions?"

Joe flashed her a breathtaking smile. "We'll just have to take it on faith."

Sure, she thought. Faith in a bunch of teenagers on a lark. Faith that none of them had gotten careless, or lazy —or curious.

"Fat chance," she muttered.

They had come to a particularly rugged part of the trail, and she trudged along behind Joe and Andrew, head down, scuffing up pine needles with the toes of her sneakers. By the time Andrew reached the top of the slope he was gasping for breath. He stopped to mop his forehead, and the moment he looked least impressive, Pete leapt from the underbrush and snapped his picture.

"Gotcha!" Pete chortled, and while Andrew stood there, huffing and puffing, blinded by the flashbulb, Peter darted back into the bushes.

When they arrived at the Coast Guard station Belle was waiting beside the monument to the victims of the *Mary Angelus* shipwreck. For the next half hour, with Joe as their guide, her cousins played follow the leader. But Cleo needed a few minutes alone.

She strolled along the bluffs above the beach while the rest of the party walked through the ruins of the barracks, and she rejoined the parade outside the charred shell of the lighthouse in time to hear the end of Joe's capsule history of the enclave.

"Chelsea Light went into operation in 1882," he was saying. "The lifeboat station was established ten years later. The Coast Guard assumed command in 1913 and stayed till the lighthouse was gutted by fire in 1918, at which point they decided to rebuild on the peninsula."

Belle said, "There's a family legend to the effect that Sam Jarman set that fire. Do you know if there's any truth to it?"

"Couldn't say," Joe answered, "but Samuel may have influenced the Coast Guard's decision to relocate. A few years earlier, he'd succeeded in buying out the fisherman who owned the original homestead on Chelsea, and I know he wanted to consolidate his holdings on the island."

"Is there anything left of the homestead?" asked Andrew.

"A cabin and several outbuildings. That's where we're headed next." Joe smiled impartially at his audience. "Is everyone ready to move on?"

Everyone was.

The trail to the homestead was less taxing than the ridge trail. For most of the distance it paralleled the shoreline, so that they could see Belle's golf cart creeping along below them.

The last few hundred yards cut through the Narrows, a thicket of stunted trees sculpted by winds that howled incessantly, even on days when the rest of Chelsea was calm. The fisherman's cabin clung like a barnacle to a slender spur of land at the extreme western tip of the island.

Cleo accompanied her cousins onto the sagging front

stoop and peered inside. Belle was enchanted by the puncheon floor, the fieldstone fireplace, the sleeping loft tucked under the eaves, but one look at the dust and cobwebs was enough for Cleo. When Joe stood to one side and motioned her to precede him, she said, "No, thanks. I think I'll sit this one out."

She did an about-face and walked away from the cabin, and Joe fell into step beside her.

"Mind if I join you?"

She shook her head and led the way past a tangle of rotting fishing nets, past crab pots warping in the salt air, toward a mound of sand and driftwood erected by the tide. In the shelter of a redwood log that had been bleached silver by the sun, she sat and watched her cousins file from the cabin to the root cellar.

"I always wondered why anyone would build here," she said. "This spot is so . . . inhospitable."

"But look at that view."

Joe was standing, looking out to sea.

"Keep this up, and I might accuse you of being a romantic," she said.

"Maybe you'd be right."

He moved one hand in a broad, sweeping gesture that took in the cabin and its lean-to, the tumbledown stable and toolshed, all built of logs, with beach grass growing along the edges of their roofs like inverted beards.

"Whenever I see all this, I can imagine what the island must've been like a hundred years ago. Beautiful, but remote. Untamed. Unforgiving. This afternoon everything's peaceful, but if a man takes the serenity for granted, he's likely to find himself in deep trouble. I guess what I'm trying to say is, it's challenging."

91

Joe glanced down at her and laughed softly. "Kind of like you, Cleo."

"You're seeing challenges where none exist," she replied. "Just because I'm not ruled by my emotions—"

"I'm surprised you'll admit you have any emotions, you try so hard to deny them." Joe sat on his heels beside her, his face watchful and intent. "What happened to you, Cleo? You were never easy to understand, even when you were a kid, but now you're completely sealed off. It's like you feel threatened if anyone gets too close."

" 'Anyone' meaning you, I suppose?" The sun was warm, but suddenly she felt chilly. She wished she had brought her sweatshirt. Her thin cotton tank top didn't offer much protection from the wind—or from Joe's gaze. Could he see how much she wanted to touch him?

She scooped up a handful of sand and let it trickle through her fingers. "Don't flatter yourself, Joe," she said, "You're assuming I'm hiding something—"

"Assuming, hell! I know you are, Cleo. And before we leave Chelsea, I intend to find out what it is."

They returned to the lodge via Treasure Bay and the trail through the woods where trillium grew. At sunset they arrived at the lily pond, with its humpbacked bridge and moon gate, and the brief golden twilight had faded into dusk before they approached the carriage house.

"This section used to be the stable," Joe explained as he unlocked one set of oversize Dutch doors. "Now it's a storeroom."

Peter rushed through the doors as soon as Joe swung them open. "Watch your step," Joe cautioned. He touched the light switch and Pete skidded to a stop.

"Hey, look at all this junk!"

Andrew let out a long, low whistle, and Tiffany said, "Holy *merde*," and disappeared inside.

"Gracious," Belle murmured, hurrying after Tiffany. "A person could spend a week in this room and not see everything."

This was only a slight exaggeration. From foundation to rafters, the storeroom was filled with the detritus of bygone days. There were enough gardening implements and carpentry tools to stock a small hardware store. There was a riding mower and a pony cart with padded leather seats and yellow wheels. There were kerosene lanterns, saddles and bridles, horse collars and buggy whips, an anvil and bellows. One corner held the spillover of castoffs from the lodge: a rocking horse, a doll carriage, golf clubs, a butter churn, a croquet set. The windows were blocked by a Ping-Pong table, which was balanced on one end against a glass-fronted trophy case.

Andrew stood in the doorway, smiling with some bemusement. "Lucille will be sorry she missed this. She's an antiques buff, like Belle."

"Then Belle should find plenty to interest her here," said Joe.

"What's next door?" Andrew asked.

"A garage."

"Is it as chock full of stuff as the storage room?"

"No. There's space for three cars, but the Hudson's the only car in it just now."

"My father used to drive a Hudson," Andrew said, an undercurrent of excitement in his voice. "What model is it?"

"Hornet, I think. Like to have a look at it?"

"Would I!"

93

The two men started toward the garage. "Coming, Cleo?" Joe called over his shoulder.

"Thanks anyway," she answered without hesitation, "but I think I'll see about dinner."

CHAPTER SEVEN

At nine o'clock that evening the party gathered in the library, where Joe was attaching a video recorder to a wide-screen TV.

"We gonna see a movie?" asked Pete.

"Not now," Joe answered. "Later, maybe."

While Joe hooked up the VCR, Andrew arranged a semicircle of chairs facing the screen and Cleo served coffee and liqueurs. Pete browsed through Elspeth's selection of movies.

"She have any Rambo?" he asked.

"If she did, it'd be there on the shelf," said Joe.

Pete ran one finger along the line of cassettes, reading the titles aloud. *Citizen Kane, Strangers on a Train, Meet Me in St. Louis—*"

"Classics," said Belle.

"Couldn't prove it by me," Pete replied, unimpressed.

"If you haven't seen 'em, don't knock 'em," Belle admonished him good-naturedly.

Pete read a few more titles, then said, "Here's one I've heard of. *It's a Wonderful Life.* Wasn't that on last Christmas?"

"It's on every Christmas," said Tiffany. "I've seen it about a million times."

Pete made a face at his sister and moved from Elspeth's movie library to the shelves, which held the complete works of Agatha Christie and Dashiell Hammet. There, between *Ten Little Indians* and *The Dain Curse,* a row of slim, leather-bound volumes caught his eye.

"Lookat this! *The Amorous Adventures of the Lustful Turk, My Secret Life, Confessions of a Courtesan—*"

He pulled one of the novels off the shelf and Tiffany rushed at her brother and made a grab for the novel he was holding.

"Lemme see," she cried.

"No way!" Pete resisted, and a tug-of-war ensued, each of them grappling for possession of the novel.

"Cut it out, you two," Andrew scolded. "That's no way to treat a book."

"Especially that book." Holding out one hand, Belle said firmly, "Give it to me, young man."

"But I wasn't—"

"Give it to me," Belle repeated. Her tone was crisp and determined enough that Peter recognized it would be futile to argue. He wrenched the book out of Tiffany's grasp and passed it to Belle.

"Just as I thought," she said, smoothing a few dog-eared pages. "It's an illustrated edition of *Fanny Hill.*"

"*Fanny Hill?*" Andrew inquired uneasily. "Isn't that pornography?"

Belle held the book toward the lamplight, studying the frontispiece from several different angles. "It's graphic," she said, "but I wouldn't call it porn."

"It's probably quite valuable," said Cleo.

Andrew raised his eyebrows. "Valuable or not, what's a book like that doing here?"

"It's from Aunt Elspeth's collection of Victorian erotica."

Andrew's eyebrows shot to a level of shocked disapproval, but before he could say anything, Joe announced that the tape was ready to roll.

Belle closed *Fanny Hill* and placed it on the table beside the lamp, and Tiffany and Peter took their chairs. Cleo sat off to one side and Joe sat next to her. An air of hushed expectancy settled over the room as Elspeth's image appeared on the screen.

She was lying in a hospital bed, looking into a hand mirror, applying the finishing touches to her makeup.

"Remember left profile's my best shot."

She spoke to someone off camera, and the answer came in a flat nasal twang.

"Sure thing."

A nurse approached the bedside, and after fussing with the scarf she had tied gypsy fashion around her head, Elspeth handed the nurse the mirror.

"I should have worn my wig," she fretted.

"Don't worry about it," said the nurse. "You look very nice."

"I look old," Elspeth insisted. "Even older than I feel."

"Ready whenever you are," the cameraman prompted.

Elspeth stared into the lens. "You're already taping."

"Gotta have the camera back by three."

Elspeth sighed and lay back against the pillows, marshaling her thoughts. She did look old, and much more fragile than Cleo remembered. The bright splotches of rouge on her cheeks accentuated her gauntness and her pallor, but her eyes hadn't changed. They were clear, and there was a poignant sparkle in them, as if she were astonished to find her blithe and ageless spirit trapped in a decaying body.

"C'mon lady," the cameraman urged. "I haven't got all day. This ain't *Gone With the Wind,* ya know."

"Not to you, maybe, but it is to me. I'd like my relatives to remember me vividly, if not with fondness." Elspeth smiled, and her features dissolved in a network of wrinkles. "Perhaps I should start by getting the rituals out of the way."

"Good plan," said the cameraman.

Elspeth acknowledged his reply with a regal nod of her head and turned to face the camera. "Good evening," she said. "I'm delighted all of you came to my party and I hope, while you're my guests, you'll consider Chelsea home. I also hope you'll be amused by the entertainment I've planned.

"By now Joe will have told you about the treasure hunt in general terms. Since he knows me as well as anyone does, he's agreed to stay on during your visit and referee the hunt. All that's left for me to explain are a few specifics. I thought about writing them down, but the ham in me preferred videotape. Besides," she confided with a chuckle, "I've always enjoyed a party, and this way I feel as if I'm one of you."

She slanted a how'm-I-doing? glance toward the cameraman, then refocused on the lens.

"Since this get-together is supposed to be fun, I've kept the rules to a minimum. In fact, there are only two. First, I've hidden my treasure somewhere on the island. And second, whoever unravels the trail of clues I've left and finds the treasure may keep it all if they wish. Of course, I hope the competition won't become too fierce. I'd hate for any of you to do anything you might regret. I'd much prefer that you agree to share and share alike. But the choice is yours. Whatever each of you decide to do is between you and your conscience."

Elspeth stopped to catch her breath. She tried to clear her throat, holding a lace-edged handkerchief to her lips, and she was seized by a paroxysm of coughing that racked her frail body. The nurse hurried to the bedside, a tumbler of water in hand, and Elspeth raised herself on one elbow to drink through the straw. After a sip or two, she collapsed against the pillows, her face ashen and strained.

"I think you'd better leave now," the nurse said to the cameraman. "She's had about all the excitement she can take."

Elspeth clutched the nurse's wrist. "Please don't run him off. I'll rest more comfortably when everything's taken care of."

"Well, at least let me start your oxygen."

"Not yet. The tube's so ugly."

"But the doctor left orders—"

"Give me another minute. That should wrap this up. Then I'll do whatever you want me to do. I promise."

Elspeth produced another smile, for both the nurse's benefit and the camera, as she said, "If Flo Ziegfeld were directing this vignette, he'd call for a drumroll here. Since this is a low-budget production, however, I'd like all of you to imagine one. And Joe, darlin', if you have your pencil and notebook, you might want to write down this next bit."

Cleo leaned forward in her chair. The silence in the library was so profound, she could hear her heart beating. She kept her eyes fixed on the screen, yet she was aware of Joe lounging in the chair beside hers, aware that he had propped a small spiral notebook on his knee and uncapped his pen.

"And now, if everybody's ready, here's the message you've been waiting for." Elspeth paused again, this time for dramatic effect, and then, in a hoarse whisper, she delivered her exit lines. "From sunrise to sunset, by the darkness of noon. Where the fair wind joins the brazen band, you'll find your first clue."

One of Elspeth's hands fluttered to her throat. With the other, she beckoned the nurse. Her shoulders sagged with weariness, yet she managed a farewell smile as her image faded and the screen went blank.

"Show's over," said Tiffany.

"It can't be," Andrew protested. "Perhaps the tape is broken."

Joe rose and turned the TV off. "I'm afraid that's it."

"But she didn't tell us anything."

"I wouldn't say that, Andrew," Belle commented. "Seems to me she told us quite a lot. Maybe even too much. Her message suggests any number of places to look for the clue."

"Yeah?" Pete scoffed. "Name one."

"Not so fast, young man," Belle demurred. "I believe our first order of business is to decide how we're going to handle this."

"You mean the split?" said Tiffany.

"Let's not put the cart before the horse," said Andrew. "We have to find the treasure before we can split it."

"Exactly," said Belle. "But are we going to tackle this thing separately or work together?"

"I vote we work together," Tiffany replied.

"Me too," said Pete.

Andrew nodded agreement, and Belle glanced at Cleo. "What about you, dear? Are you in or out?"

"I'll go along with whatever arrangement the rest of you prefer."

"Good for you," said Belle. "Assuming Joe has no objections, that makes it unanimous."

"Wait a minute," Joe said. "Are you suggesting I should have a share of the treasure?"

"It's only fair," Belle answered. "You've devoted more time to this hunt than anyone else."

"But you heard Elspeth's instructions. I'm here as an adviser. Besides, I'm not a Jarman."

"But without you, none of us would be here, so either we're in this together or it's winner take all."

"Belle's right," said Andrew. "If we don't pool our resources, it's possible none of us will find the treasure."

"After this afternoon's tour, I'd say the odds are against our finding it," Belle declared cheerfully. "So it's up to you, Joe."

He gave her a lopsided grin. "Since you put it that way, how can I refuse."

"Then it's settled," said Belle. "Whatever Elspeth's treasure is, we'll divide it even-Steven when we find it."

"*If* we find it," Tiffany qualified somberly.

"Yeah," Pete said with some consternation, as if he were dismayed to find himself agreeing with his sister twice in the same evening. "Where do we begin?"

"With Elspeth's poem," Belle replied. "Let's listen to it one more time and then we can make a list of any hiding places it brings to mind."

"Would you like me to run the tape again?" asked Joe.

The thought of watching an instant replay of her aunt's suffering was repugnant to Cleo, and she spoke up before Belle could answer. "Why don't you just read us the poem?"

"That's the ticket," said Andrew. "If we put our heads together and approach this thing logically, we'll solve Elspeth's riddle in no time."

Cleo doubted logic would be much help—Elspeth had not been a logical woman—but she kept her reservations to herself while Joe reread her aunt's poem and the others made their own copies of it.

Andrew thought the first line might be a reference to the song "Sunrise, Sunset," from *Fiddler on the Roof.* Joe said that interpretation certainly would be consistent with Elspeth's fondness for musical comedy, and Andrew rushed off to scout the exterior of the house and check the outline of the roof.

He returned to the library ten minutes later, limping and rubbing his leg. "Banged my shin on some kind of lawn ornament," he announced. "I'm afraid it's broken."

"Your leg?" Belle inquired anxiously.

"No. That damn plastic flamingo or whatever it was I tripped over."

"What about the roof?" asked Belle.

"Can't say for sure. It's dark as a cave out there, so I couldn't see much, but there is a weather vane on one of the peaks. I'll have a closer look in the morning."

"A weather vane would fit the part about 'Where the fair wind joins the brazen band,'" said Tiffany.

"There's also a sundial on the back terrace, near the fountain," said Belle. "That would fit both 'sunrise to sunset' and 'darkness of noon.'"

"And there's the sailboat," said Tiffany. "It's named *Fair Wind.*"

"Good girl," said Belle, adding the sailboat to her list.

"Isn't 'brazen' an old-time way of saying brass?" asked Pete.

Andrew stopped rubbing his shin and beamed at the boy. "Yes, son, it is."

"Then maybe we should be looking for a violin or a trumpet."

"Or the whole orchestra," said Tiffany.

"Or a record album." Pete's voice was shrill with excitement as he asked Joe, "Didn't Elspeth have a music room somewhere on this floor?"

"Two doors down," Joe answered. With Pete and Tiffany on their way to the hall, he continued, "You'll find the instruments in their cases, and records in the cabinets—"

The door slammed and Pete and Tiffany were gone, and Cleo added quietly, "Part of her collection's in the parlor, but it's mostly older stuff—Billie Holiday and Louis Armstrong."

"Don't forget the waltzes," said Joe.

Cleo flushed and looked away from him, wishing she could forget the way they had waltzed. The warmth of his arms about her, the sweetness of his breath upon her cheek, the hard strength of his body close to hers . . .

"Obviously, we can't search outdoors till tomorrow," Belle said, "but Elspeth's poem suggests a couple of likely hiding spots right in this room."

"I know one of them," Andrew said, scanning the books on the shelves. "There's a novel by Arthur Koestler titled *Darkness at Noon.*"

"I hadn't thought of that, but 'sunrise to sunset' could be Elspeth's way of saying east and west."

"The atlas," said Andrew.

"Or the globe," Belle concluded.

In an instant, Cleo's cousins were scurrying off to investigate these prospects, and for the first time since their walk on the beach near the fisherman's shack, Cleo and Joe had a moment of privacy.

"You don't seem very enthusiastic," Joe observed in an undertone only Cleo could hear.

"I'm not," she admitted.

"Why? Are you so positive the treasure's a myth?"

"No, it's more . . . Well, maybe it's just that the videotape was disappointing."

"Were you expecting a personal message?"

Cleo pressed her lips together and didn't answer.

"She didn't know whether I'd find you, Cleo."

"I realize it doesn't make sense, Joe, but still, I'd hoped . . ." Tears stung Cleo's eyes and she blinked them back. "The other thing is, Aunt Elspeth was always so vital. It was sad to see her dependent on others."

"Her mind was sharp though," Joe said. "She managed to run the show, right to the end."

"I wonder if she's still running it."

Joe followed Cleo's gaze toward the opposite end of the room, where Belle and Andrew were rummaging through Elspeth's library.

"What's to wonder? Looks to me as if everyone's following Elspeth's game plan."

"So far," Cleo said. "But what's going to happen in a day or two?"

"I take it you don't think your cousins will abide by their bargain."

"Do you?"

Joe shrugged. "They seem sincere."

"Of course they do. This early in the game they have everything to gain by cooperating with each other and nothing to lose but their good intentions. But it won't last, Joe. Sooner or later, someone's going to get greedy, and when that happens, watch out. It'll be every man for himself."

Now it was Joe who seemed skeptical.

"Evidently you don't agree," Cleo said.

"Oh, I'm willing to grant you may be right. The closer we get to finding the treasure, the more likely it becomes that one or more of us will decide to invoke the winner-take-all rule."

"Then why are you staring at me that way?"

"What way?"

"Don't play dumb with me, Joe Gamble. You know perfectly well you've been looking at me as if I were a bug under a microscope."

A mote of anger erupted in Joe's eyes. "That's part of your trouble, lady. You're too damn suspicious for your own good."

"Listen, I know when I'm being stared at."

"All right, Cleo. Maybe I was staring, but it wasn't intentional. I was thinking how deceptive appearances can be. Anyone seeing you for the first time would think you're all softness and innocence, but nothing could be further from the truth. You're as cynical as they come."

"So what's your point?"

"Just that you must find life pretty grim if you always expect the worst from people."

"At least I'm rarely disappointed."

Joe gave her a probing glance, then shook his head. "I don't buy that. My guess is you're constantly disappointed. I suspect what you really want is for somebody to prove you're wrong, that it's safe for you to give a damn about someone besides yourself."

Cleo returned his gaze stoically, her face stiff with composure. "You're entitled to your opinion, Joe. That doesn't mean I have to defend myself, and I certainly don't have to sit here and listen to you."

She got to her feet and started for the door. She had almost reached the hall when Joe fired a parting shot.

"I feel sorry for you, Cleo."

"Don't waste your sympathy on me, Joe. I don't need it."

She responded evenly, without looking back. Her step never faltered as she crossed the foyer and climbed the stairs. Unlike the night twelve years before when she had eavesdropped on Joe and Steffi, on this night she had not permitted Joe to have the last word.

She had acquitted herself well. She had told Joe she didn't want his pity. She'd kept her cool. She hadn't flinched. Perhaps she hadn't won the argument, but she hadn't lost it either.

So why did she feel defeated?

CHAPTER EIGHT

The sound of someone knocking at her door roused Cleo from a deep, dreamless sleep the next morning. She mumbled a protest, clinging to oblivion until the rapping was repeated.

She had never found it easy to socialize before she'd had coffee, and on this particular morning, the last thing she wanted was a friendly wake-up call from one or another of her cousins. She reacted instinctively, pulling the covers over her head. If she ignored the knocking, maybe her visitor would go away.

Less than a minute later, the noise came again, more insistent than before.

"Who is it?" she called.

The only answer was pounding loud enough to shake the walls and ceiling of her room. She bolted to a sitting position and squinted crossly at the door.

"Keep your shirt on. I'm coming."

The bedclothes were tangled about her legs. Her dressing gown had vanished in the snarl. One end of the belt trailed over the footboard, but before she could find the rest of the robe, the knocking resumed.

"Just a minute," she called.

Her efforts to free the robe had only tangled it more

tightly in the bedclothes. Suddenly aware of a dull ache in her temples, she cursed the brilliant morning light, her visitor, and the grogginess that made her fingers feel swollen and uncoordinated. Most of all, she cursed the incessant pounding.

She clamped her hands over her ears to muffle the din. "Damn," she muttered. "This is like being trapped inside a bass drum."

She gave up searching for the dressing gown and stumbled toward the door, but when she opened it, no one was there. She rubbed her eyes and peered into the hallway.

The corridor was dark and cool. It was also deserted.

More alert now, she realized that the noise was coming from somewhere above her; from the attic perhaps, or even the roof.

And then she remembered the weather vane.

She rushed to her bedroom window, threw it open, and stepped onto the little balcony outside. Her cousins were clustered on the terrace two stories below, staring up at the roof with openmouthed fascination. The third floor cornice prevented her from seeing what they were watching. Even when she leaned over the balcony railing she could not see the roof, but she knew very well that Joe must be up there, making the climb to the weather vane.

She envisioned the steep pitch of the roof, and her stomach knotted with fear.

In the next moment she was running, out of her room and along the hall, down the stairs to the foyer. The front door was ajar, and she didn't stop to close it. She raced along the veranda and across the lawn to the terrace.

She caught her first glimpse of Joe when she rounded the corner of the house. Reaching the fountain she hopped onto the stone rim that circled the base, where she had an unimpeded view of Joe. She watched, panic-stricken.

He was working at a dizzying height near the peak of the third floor roof, nailing narrow strips of pine onto the shingles, using the strips as toeholds as he made his way toward the weather vane.

"Can you see anything?" Andrew shouted.

"Not yet," Joe answered.

Cleo wanted to scream at him to come down from his perch, but her vocal cords refused to function. She could only watch and offer mute prayers for his safety as he withdrew another strip of pine from his backpack and hammered it on to the roof.

The next few minutes passed in an agony of tension. Cleo focused on Joe, monitoring his slightest movement as if her powers of concentration could keep him from falling. Aside from Joe, the only detail she saw with any clarity was the figure on the weather vane: a dainty mermaid whose hair streamed over her shoulders and whose outstretched arms embraced the breeze.

Cleo held her breath while Joe nailed the last wooden rungs in place; her prayers became more fervent as he inched upward and planted his feet on either side of the ridgeline. He braced himself for the final assault, and with one fluid motion, he straightened.

For a moment she saw him poised there, his body erect and triumphant against the sky, and then she couldn't take any more. She closed her eyes and kept them shut while Andrew asked Joe what he had found.

"Bird droppings," Joe answered.

Andrew chuckled. Cleo whispered, "Climb down, Joe. Please climb down."

She didn't risk another glance at him until he had begun his descent, and as his safety became more certain, awareness returned.

Belle and Andrew were standing by the sundial, planning the day's search. Tiffany was combing her hair—today she'd colored it fluorescent orange. Pete was snapping pictures. Between shots, Cleo caught him ogling her legs, and that reminded her that the nightshirt she was wearing was something less than modest.

She scrambled off the fountain and hurried toward the house before anyone else could see her.

Her equanimity was intact and the house was quiet half an hour later when, showered and dressed in a blue and white camisole dress, ready to confront the day, she wandered into the kitchen.

She had hoped to find breakfast; instead she found Joe.

He was sitting at the table, enjoying his second cup of coffee and looking unperturbed, as if he spent every morning defying gravity.

Cleo's hand shook as she poured coffee for herself. "Where are the others?" she asked.

"At the landing. They wanted to check out the *Fair Wind.*"

She nodded and put bread into the toaster. "Shouldn't you be keeping an eye on them?"

"What for?"

"They might get lost."

"On an island?"

She heard amusement in Joe's voice and gritted her teeth, vowing that from now on she would think before she spoke.

"I presume no one's found anything," she said.

"They haven't found the clue, if that's what you mean, but I made an interesting discovery." Joe paused, giving

110

her the chance to comment, but instead of asking what he'd found, she remained silent. "Wouldn't you like to know what it is?"

"Not especially, but I'll bet you're going to tell me."

"Better than that, Cleo. I'm going to show you." Joe removed a photograph from his shirt pocket and slid it across the tabletop. "Go on," he said. "Take a look."

"Why bother? I imagine it's a snapshot Pete took of me."

"Right. And what a snapshot!"

Joe retrieved the picture and made a great show of comparing the woman in the photograph with the flesh-and-blood original, but somewhere along the way, he forgot his intention to tease Cleo. And no wonder. In the picture she was wearing a thigh-length nightdress that was tailored like a man's shirt, but on her it looked delectably feminine and downright sexy. Her alluring sleepwear accounted for only part of his interest in the photo, however.

Pete had captured Cleo in a rare moment of candor, with all her attention on Joe's climb to the weather vane. The sheer, clingy fabric of the nightshirt disclosed most of her secrets, the objective lens of the Polaroid bared the rest, and for the first time, Joe saw through her detachment. He saw that she had been frightened for him, and realized that her cool demeanor was an act. She might seem aloof and self-contained, as if she cared for no one but herself, but the anxiety he saw in her pale, delicate features *proved* it was an act. He marveled that he had been taken in. He was a professional, trained to look for the unexpected, yet Cleo had fooled him. He could almost applaud her bravura performance.

Smiling with admiration, he said, "This picture's very

111

revealing, Cleo. It's made me see you in a totally new light."

He's baiting me, Cleo thought, toying with me. But she'd had enough of his cat-and-mouse tactics. Her fingers clenched around the handle of the butter knife, but aside from that she remained impassive.

"I'd like to have my breakfast in peace, Joe. If there's some point to this conversation, I'd appreciate your making it."

She underscored her indifference by returning to the toaster, but that was a mistake. In an instant Joe was at her back, his hands propped on the counter at either side of her, blocking her retreat.

"I'm on to you, Cleo. I know you care for me."

He sounded so macho, so sure of himself. His arrogance left her gasping. "Of all the conceited—"

"Your secret's safe with me, honey. You don't have to pretend anymore."

His chest vibrated against her shoulder blades when he spoke. His breath gusted over the sensitive skin at the nape of her neck in a hot, exciting caress.

She tried not to respond. She didn't *want* to respond, but it seemed she couldn't help herself. His lips roved over her bare shoulder, and the fine, downy hairs on her forearms stood on end. His arms curved about her waist, gathering her close, and her body went soft and yielding against his.

"Please, Joe, I can't—"

"Trust me, Cleo. You know I'd never do anything to hurt you."

She wanted to protest that she knew nothing of the sort, but she couldn't find her voice. She felt the tantalizing warmth of his lips against her throat, her earlobe, her chin, her cheek, and once again her woman's body betrayed her.

She turned slightly in his arms, and a tiny mewing sound escaped her as he kissed her mouth, a feather touch, barely grazing her lips with his.

Brief though it was, the contact was intoxicating, and he kissed her again, less hastily. By the third kiss she had closed her eyes and wrapped her arms about his neck, and this time his mouth settled over hers even more slowly.

He took his time, brushing his lips from side to side with moist, nibbling, prying motions, coaxing her response. She opened her mouth and clung to him, and Joe widened his stance. He distributed her weight against him, shaping her body to his, supporting her effortlessly. His arms closed about her more tightly, his hold became stronger, harder, more eager. The pressure of his mouth ranged from teasing to frankly desirous to hot and hungry and urgent, and she was lost in sensation, lost in pleasure so intense it seemed boundless.

Desire overcame apprehension. Reason drifted away. She gloried in the feel of Joe's hands upon her, in the demands of his mouth and the sweet ravishment of his tongue. She heard his ragged breathing and the hoarse endearments he crooned. She heard his heart racing, keeping counterpoint to hers. But she did not hear the front door open. Nor did she hear Belle's "*Yoo*-hoo. Is anybody home?"

Joe did, however. He lifted his head and froze, listening to footsteps crossing the foyer.

"Something's burning." Tiffany's voice came from the dining room, just beyond the kitchen, and reality intruded.

113

Cleo sprang away from Joe a fraction of a second before her cousins burst into the kitchen, but once inside the room they stopped to fan whorls of smoke away from their eyes.

"Gracious!" Belle cried. "What's going on in here?"

Cleo drew in a deep, shaky breath, and the odor of burned toast filled her nostrils. Joe was busy opening windows, and choking and coughing, her eyes watering, she made a blind attempt to unplug the toaster. Instead of the cord, she grabbed the overheated metal at the top of the appliance and yelped with pain.

"Everything's under control," Joe said, herding Belle and Tiffany through the door. "Why don't you ladies wait in the parlor till the smoke clears."

"But we wanted to let you know—"

He shut the door in Belle's dumbfounded face. Apparently, Joe decided whatever Belle wanted to tell him could wait until he and Cleo had another minute alone. Her startled "Well, I never . . ." followed him as he hurried to the sink, where Cleo was running cold water over her scorched fingers.

"Let's have a look," he said. He reached for Cleo's wrist, but she pulled away.

"I'm all right," she said.

"Are you sure?"

"Positive." Her fingertips smarted a bit, but considering that she'd been playing with fire, that seemed a small price to pay. "Maybe you should join Belle and Tiffany. In fact, I wish you would."

His eyes narrowed with speculation. "Is that supposed to be a brush-off?"

"Yes, it is."

"It won't work, honey. Not after what just happened

114

between us. But I will give you time to think it over." He turned to leave the kitchen, then hesitated. "About that picture . . ."

"Yes? What about it?"

"You tell me. What do you want me to do with it?"

Cleo turned off the tap and dried her hands. Her voice trembled with outrage as she said, "It would give me great satisfaction to tear it in little pieces and flush it down the john."

Joe shrugged. "Seems like a waste of a perfectly good snapshot, but if you want it, it's yours."

Her eyes widened with surprise at this unprecedented kindness. "Thank you, Joe. That's very considerate of you."

"Don't mention it."

"But I'd like you to know I'm grateful."

Joe gave a soft chuckle. "No need to be. I have a couple of others."

Before Cleo could find something to throw at him, Joe pushed through the door and left the room, but the sound of his laughter mocked her long after he had gone.

CHAPTER NINE

Cleo never did have breakfast that day. She was too upset to eat, and since she didn't feel up to exchanging pleasantries with her cousins, she went out the back door and spent the rest of the morning in the grape arbor, fuming at Joe and thinking of the hateful things she would say to him, if only he were there.

She'd shown a smidgen of concern for his welfare, and wham! he was convinced she'd welcome his advances. He probably thought she was in love with him, for heaven's sake, but she wasn't. At least, she *hoped* she wasn't. . . .

Good lord, she couldn't be! The last thing she needed was to fall in love with Joe Gamble. He'd dredged up the past, shattered her contentment, and turned her safe, orderly world upside down. He had subjected her to storms at sea, terrified her with his daredevil stunts, and then, to top it all off, he'd had the gall to make a pass at her. More than anything else, she wished he were with her in the arbor so she could tell him how much she *didn't* love him.

She half hoped he would come looking for her, and that he didn't added to her fury.

When she returned to the house she found Belle in the

kitchen, filling a wicker hamper with sandwiches and cold chicken.

"There you are, dear," she said. "We've been hunting all over for you."

This was news to Cleo. In the hours she'd spent in the arbor, she hadn't seen a soul. "Did you find my aunt's clue?" she asked.

"Not yet, but I'm sure we will soon," Belle answered confidently. "Joe suggested we take a break, so we're having a picnic at Treasure Bay, and we wondered if you'd like to come with us."

Cleo thanked Belle for the invitation, but declined. The flushed, feverish sensation that shot through her at the mention of Joe's name made her wonder if she might be coming down with something.

She went up the back stairs to the bathroom adjoining her bedroom and splashed cold water on her face. This soothed her stinging cheeks, but to be on the safe side, she chose to stay in her room till her cousins had left for the beach.

She watched their departure from the balcony window. Andrew and Pete, under Belle's supervision, loaded a golf cart with the picnic basket, a cooler and portable grill, the volleyball net, and a stack of towels and blankets. Their preparations complete, Andrew and Belle got into the cart and headed toward the beach, with Pete following on foot.

The dust had scarcely settled when Joe and Tiffany came out of the house and set off across the lawn, and Cleo watched them until they moved out of sight. They were talking and laughing, having such a good time that she felt a pang of envy. She was tempted to run after them, tell them she'd changed her mind about the picnic—

She recalled Pete's snapshot, and stiffened her spine, resolving not to give in to temptation. She wasn't a starry-eyed teenager anymore, and she preferred a few hours of loneliness to the hazards of tagging along with Joe.

Besides, now that she had the house to herself, there was one place she wanted to look for Elspeth's clue.

She had thought Pete and Tiffany were on the right track when they went off to search the music room. "Where the fair wind joins the brazen band" did suggest an orchestra. It suggested clarinets and trumpets in particular. And so far, no one had checked the big brass trumpet on the Victrola.

At least, she didn't think anyone had checked it.

Joe had used the Victrola the evening of their arrival, of course, but the parlor had been dark. If the clue was another of Elspeth's poems, and if it were taped inside the bell, it could have escaped his notice.

As Cleo hurried toward the parlor, she imagined the others returning from the beach. She imagined greeting them with the announcement that she had solved her aunt's riddle. Her cousins would be delighted and Joe amazed when she presented them with the clue.

She was so certain she was right, she couldn't believe her eyes when she examined the trumpet and found nothing. She looked again, ran one hand over the dusty surface of the bell, and peered inside it again.

Still nothing.

Had one of her cousins beat her to it? Had Peter and Tiffany discovered the clue and kept it to themselves?

And what about Joe?

Last night, after he'd run the videotape, the others had plunged into the hunt, but Joe had been restrained and enigmatic, as if he knew something the rest of the party didn't know. Now Cleo wondered if he did. Like everyone else, she had believed that since her aunt had trusted him to organize the house party, Joe must be a man of principle. But what if he wasn't? What if he'd used his access to the tape to his own advantage? With that kind of head start, he might have found the treasure weeks ago. . . .

No, wait! Cleo thought. If Joe had found the treasure, he wouldn't have contacted me. He'd have canceled the house party, I'd have been none the wiser, and the Jarmans would never have suspected a thing.

And she'd forgotten the inventory Elspeth had deposited with her lawyer. Surely that left Joe in the clear.

But where does it leave me? Cleo wondered.

She was trying to make sense of all this when a gnawing sensation in the pit of her stomach reminded her she'd had nothing to eat since yesterday's dinner. She wandered into the kitchen and stood at the refrigerator, confused and uncertain, unable to decide what she wanted.

"I'm still not hungry," she said.

She poured a glass of milk and forced herself to drink it, sitting at the table, staring at the clock on the wall. Ten minutes crept by, so sluggishly they seemed like an hour.

"I should've gone on the picnic," she said.

She was standing at the sink, rinsing her glass, when Pete dashed into the kitchen. Her first thought was that he'd been delegated to check up on her, that her cousins didn't trust her any more than she trusted them. But despite her suspicions, she was relieved to see him.

119

"Back so soon?" she said.

"Forgot the volleyball. Joe said you'd know where to find it."

"There used to be a box of sports equipment in the attic." She put the glass in the dishwasher and added, "C'mon. I'll show you."

Cleo hadn't ventured into the attic since her return. Judging by the layer of dust on the floor, no one else had either. Not for months—maybe years. It was much as she remembered, only more so: a rabbit warren of cubicles, filled with boxes and trunks, broken furniture and cobwebs. She and Pete walked single file through a maze of mover's cartons until they reached the largest storeroom. The smell of mildew made her sneeze. She turned on the overhead light, but it did little to dispel the gloom.

Pete looked about and nervously cleared his throat. "We should've left a trail of bread crumbs."

Cleo's laughter seemed to startle and please him. It also restored his confidence. He swaggered to the box she indicated and tore the flaps aside. The volleyball was near the top.

"Only one problem," he said. He held the volleyball so that Cleo saw the grooves his fingertips made in the leather casing.

"There should be an air pump in the box," she said.

She pried several cartons open while Pete found the air pump. By the time he'd inflated the ball she had located the box that held her aunt's scrapbooks. She made a random selection, placed it on top of the box and opened it.

Pete gave the volleyball a bounce, testing it. The slap of leather on wood made more noise than he had anticipated, and he grimaced. Any second now, he thought, Cleo's gonna holler at me to pipe down.

She didn't, though, even when he tried the ball again.

He stole a glance at her as he pumped more air into the ball. She was thumbing through a big loose-leaf album, pausing now and then to read something.

Keeping one eye on Cleo, he gave the ball another bounce. It hit the floor with a resounding *thwack,* but she didn't seem to hear it. He tried a fourth time, testing her more than the volleyball. She did not respond.

Stymied, he bounced the ball along the floor, dribbling closer to her. It made a staccato sound, like rifle fire. He stirred up a miasma of dust that made him cough, but Cleo kept on reading.

Has she gone deaf? he wondered.

He squatted down less than three feet away from her, sitting on the ball in lieu of a chair, and considered his options.

Cleo might be deaf, but she sure wasn't blind. The storeroom was so murky, he was surprised she could read. If he'd brought his camera, he could snap her picture and the flash would get her attention. Since he had left the Polaroid at the beach, however, he tapped her on the ankle and said, " 'Scuse me."

"Yes? Are you ready to leave?"

Aggrieved, he said, "I can find my own way out."

"I never doubted it."

Cleo answered simply, one adult to another, and Pete's antagonism turned to bewilderment. He was used to being yelled at. He could handle Belle's meddling, his father's preaching, his sister's insults, and his mother's nagging, but Cleo had him baffled. She treated him as if he were a grown-up, not a bratty kid, and he didn't know how to respond to that.

He grinned sheepishly and wound his arms around his

legs. After a protracted silence he asked, "Is that one of Elspeth's scrapbooks?"

"Yes, it is."

"Could I read it when you're through?"

"What about the volleyball game?"

"I meant afterwards."

"Help yourself," Cleo said. "This box is full of my aunt's scrapbooks."

"No kidding?"

She closed the album and lifted it to one side so that he could see for himself.

"Awesome," he said.

"I think so, too."

Cleo smiled at him, and he could feel his ears turning red. "You sure you don't mind me reading them?" he asked.

"Why should I mind?"

"My dad says there are some things you might be sensitive about. He told me not to mention 'em."

"So naturally you got curious."

"Yeah," Pete admitted grudgingly, just realizing this himself. "How'd you know?"

"As I said, it's natural. Besides, I was your age once." Cleo seemed a little sad, but not at all annoyed. She traced the scrollwork on the album cover with her forefinger as she murmured, "I was about your age when I found this scrapbook. I was fascinated by it—read it straight through."

"Did you read the others?"

"Not all of them, no."

He scooted closer to her. "If you'd like, I could carry that box downstairs. Then you could take your time

122

. . ." Cleo shook her head, and he left the rest of his offer unspoken.

"Thanks, anyway," she said, "but I'm not sure I want to spend much time with them."

"Well, if that's the way you want it." Pete got to his feet and scooped up the volleyball. "Let me know if you change your mind."

"All right, Pete. I will."

He bounce-passed the ball to her and she swatted it back to him. "Know something, Cleo. You and my sister are a lot alike."

"In what way?"

"You both hide your feelings." Cleo's frown warned him he was treading on thin ice, but he persisted. "Tiffany acts like she hates it here, but the truth is, she was real excited about meeting you."

"How do you know she was?"

"I heard her talking to her boyfriend, bragging about having relatives with connections in Hollywood."

"That's not me, Pete. That's my mother and father and Aunt Elspeth."

"But you must've met some of their friends."

"Yes, years ago. But since my mother's death, my connection with show business has been strictly as a spectator."

"That's good enough for Tiffany."

"Very well," said Cleo. "I'm willing to concede you may be right about your sister, but you're way off target about me. I don't hide my feelings."

"Sure you do, Cleo. I don't want to make you mad or anything, but at first I thought you were sorta stuck up. You acted as if this house party was a big pain, and I got

123

the impression you'd decided not to like the rest of us before you ever met us."

"But now you've changed your mind?"

"Yeah. Now I think you're shy."

"And *I* think you're too young to play psychologist."

"Get real, Cleo. You're steamed right now, and doin' your best not to show it. That *proves* what I've been saying."

He's wrong, Cleo thought. Of course he's wrong.

But for the life of her, she couldn't think of a single argument that would convince Pete he was mistaken.

CHAPTER TEN

"What did you do to Pete?"

Joe's quietly voiced question was the last straw. Cleo threw down her napkin, piled her cup and saucer onto her dessert plate, gathered up her silverware, and left the dining room.

A glance around the table assured Joe no one else had noticed her abrupt departure. The morning's hunt and an afternoon of volleyball had taken their toll on Belle. She was slumped over her plate, emitting occasional ladylike snores. Andrew was scribbling notes to himself, planning tomorrow's search, and Tiffany and Peter were squabbling over the last piece of huckleberry pie.

After a hasty "Excuse me," Joe picked up his own dishes and carried them into the kitchen.

Cleo was at the sink, rinsing the dinner plates with reckless disregard for the scalding temperature of the water. She didn't turn around when Joe stepped into the room, but she seemed to know he was there. The instant he shut the swinging door, she said, "I've had all the criticism I can take."

"Criticism?" he repeated.

"You heard me. First you and your 'I'm on to you, Cleo,' then Pete and his harebrained theories." She shoved a strand of hair away from her eyes with the back of her wrist and scowled at him through a veil of steam. "This has not been a good day for me, Joe. I'm warning you, I have had it."

"Cleo, I don't know what—"

"Oh, put a sock in it." She faced him head on, brandishing the dishcloth. "The next person who accuses me of putting on an act is going to get this rag stuffed down his throat."

She hurled the dishcloth onto the counter, and began dumping silverware into the sink, hostility in every move. Joe approached her cautiously.

"How about a compliment?" he said.

"From you? Ha! Don't make me laugh. You're the one who declared the open season on Cleo Dennis."

He reached over her shoulder and turned off the tap. "Look, honey—"

"Don't 'honey' me you—you character assassin!"

She started running the water again, and he turned it off. The moment he withdrew his hand, she made a grab for the tap, but this time he was ready for her. He caught her wrist and held it tightly, so that she couldn't pull away.

"Don't touch me!" she cried.

Joe hesitated, thinking of all the ways he'd like to touch her. His gaze wandered over her, lingering on the hectic rush of color to her cheeks and her soft, pink mouth. He felt a sudden tightening in his loins and thought God! I'd like to do a lot more than touch her. He wanted to take her in his arms and bury his face in her bright tousled hair. He wanted to feel her lush, yielding mouth beneath his mouth, kiss her till she begged for

126

more, then do it all over again. He wanted to make love to her. . . .

But the low murmur of voices from the dining room reminded him this was neither the time nor the place. At any second, one of her cousins could walk in on them. When he made love to Cleo—and he was sure now that they would make love—he wanted to savor every nuance. He wanted their lovemaking to be slow and thorough, not rushed and furtive. He wanted to possess her totally.

He felt her trembling, saw the leap of the pulse in her throat, and when he met her eyes he saw a reflection of his own desire beneath the mutinous sparkle.

His grip on her wrist loosened; his touch on her arm became persuasive, seductive, a caress. He no longer held her against her will. She could walk away from him if she wanted to—but she didn't want to.

"Listen, honey," he said, "I don't know what went on between you and Pete this afternoon, but you seem to have worked some kind of miracle. Pete left the beach an unholy terror and came back almost likable. I'm not saying he's perfect. Far from it. But he seems human—like a regular kid."

"He's human, all right, but he's not a kid. He's a thirty-year-old midget!"

Joe ran a tentative finger along her cheek. "Pete really got to you, didn't he?"

Cleo shrugged.

"Want to tell me about it?" he asked.

She began stacking pots and utensils in the dishwasher. "There's not much to tell. Anyway, it's not so much what Pete said that's upsetting."

"No? Then what is?"

She shoved the frying pan onto the rack, annoyed that

Joe had to ask. "Just the idea of being analyzed by a munchkin! Pete knows zilch about life—he knows even less about me—but he feels perfectly free to interpret my behavior and make all sorts of dumb comparisons."

"What comparisons?"

"Between Tiffany and me! Can you believe it?" Joe handed her the collander and she rearranged the saucepans to make room for it. Almost as an afterthought, she added, "Pete also has this crazy notion that I'm here under protest."

Aha! Joe thought. Now we're down to the nitty-gritty. Tongue in cheek, he said, "Where do you suppose he got an idea like that?"

"Certainly not from me," Cleo snapped. "Oh, I'll admit I wasn't thrilled about this house party at first, but once I thought it over—"

I still wasn't thrilled.

She tried again. "What I mean is, even if I were here under duress, no one would guess . . ."

Except Pete. And Joe. And maybe Andrew and Tiffany.

"Besides," she continued weakly, "whatever my personal preferences, I've been pleasant."

But I haven't spent any more time with my cousins than is absolutely necessary, and I haven't gotten involved with the treasure hunt. I've observed the letter of Aunt Elspeth's last request, but not the spirit of it— which is a polite way of saying I've been putting on an act.

Cleo slid the last dinner plate into the rack and closed the dishwasher. She couldn't bring herself to look at Joe, but she sensed his gaze upon her, witnessing her emotional tug-of-war.

The same unruly strand of hair had fallen over her eyes. She started to shove it back again, but he brushed it away from her forehead and held it in place with a kiss. And then, somehow, his arms were about her waist, and she realized his touch was not at all tentative.

"Tell me honestly," she murmured, "how would you feel if Pete accused you of being shy?"

"I'd be angry."

"What if it were true?" she asked. "What if you were convinced that someone—maybe a relative—wouldn't like you, no matter how agreeable you tried to be?"

"I'd keep them at a distance, and I'd be even more angry." Joe's lips touched her cheek as he spoke, setting her alight, robbing her of reason.

She couldn't speak, could barely think. Her resistance to Joe was growing weaker by the second, and she knew that she should do something to stop him before she lost it entirely.

But his broad, powerful hands were moving over her back, creating a delicious friction as they slipped from crisp striped cotton to silken skin, and instead of trying to free herself, she relaxed against his chest.

Pete was right, she thought.

Funny, how easy it was to confront her fears when Joe was holding her in his arms.

Another storm blew in that night. Monday's dawn brought gray skies and a steady, soaking rain. At breakfast, Cleo and Joe went over Elspeth's verse line by line. They made a list of likely hiding places and concluded that the second line was the key to the riddle.

Joe said, " 'Darkness of noon' makes me think of shadows."

129

"Me too," Cleo said. "But shadows of what?"

"Your guess is as good as mine, but it's gotta be outside."

"Why do you say that?"

"Well, whatever it is, it's related to sunlight and wind."

Cleo consulted their list. "If you throw in the brass band, that narrows it down to the sundial, the weather vane, or the sailboat."

"Now we're getting somewhere!"

"I don't see how, Joe. We've already exhausted those possibilities."

He shook his head. "Not when you consider what we should've been looking for is shadows."

But for the time being they couldn't pursue this angle. As Pete pointed out, "You can't find shadows in the rain."

No one had much appetite for lunch that day, and that evening, after dinner, everyone went their separate ways.

Andrew ventured out to the carriage house for another look at the Hudson, Pete locked himself in his room with *Fanny Hill,* and Tiffany had discovered the armoire that held Elspeth's wardrobe and was experimenting with beads and bangles and flapper dresses.

Cleo had no idea where Joe was. She told herself she didn't care, but she wandered about like a lost soul until she passed Belle's room.

"Why don't you come in, dear," the older woman called.

Reluctantly, Cleo did, and they spent the evening going through a box of old photographs while Belle reminisced about her childhood and rattled more than a few family skeletons. Belle was especially pleased when she came upon a picture of herself. "That's me," she declared proudly.

"You were an adorable baby," Cleo replied, marveling that the sweet-faced cherub who resembled a Kate Greenaway illustration should have turned into a gossipy spinster like Belle.

And why, Cleo wondered, am I listening to her gossip —and enjoying it?

The answer to this remained one of life's little mysteries when another question occurred to her.

"Isn't that Aunt Elspeth holding you?"

"Indeed it is, dear."

"I didn't realize you'd met her."

"Oh, yes. She paid a visit to my parents on her way to New York. She only stayed a week, but she made quite a splash in Sandusky. She was quite an accomplished flirt, you know. I've been told some of our local young men were heartbroken when she left town."

"Is it true that she ran away from home?"

"In a way. She and her father had a falling out, and she left Chelsea against his wishes, but she defied him openly and with a certain elegance."

"Yes, she was elegant," Cleo murmured. "When was this picture taken?"

"Well, now, let me think." Belle peered at the picture through her reading glasses. "Ah, yes. This must have been the day she arrived in Sandusky. I'm ashamed to admit I gave her a soggy welcome."

"Soggy?"

"That's right, dear. I left my—er, calling card on her lap. I don't remember it, of course. I was only five months old."

"What was the occasion?"

"My christening. Perhaps you recognize the dress I was wearing. It was a lovely thing—ivory linen, hand embroidered and trimmed with yards of Belgian lace. An heirloom, really. All the Jarman babies were christened in it, including your mother."

Cleo took a closer look at the photograph. "The dress does look familiar . . ." She lapsed into silence as her attention drifted to the radiant likeness of the young Elspeth. "You know, Belle," she said. "I can't put my finger on it, but there's something very different about her."

"It's the hair," said Belle. "On Saturday night, when Joe ran the videotape, I noticed immediately that she was wearing a scarf."

"Then she wasn't always—"

"Bald? Gracious, no! You can see for yourself she had truly spectacular hair, and scads of it. In those days we called the color strawberry blonde."

"Well, what happened to it?"

"She had an illness. Influenza, I believe. It was during the epidemic in 1918, or maybe it was 1919. At any rate, she had a high fever. We heard she nearly died."

"And that's when she lost her hair?"

"Yes, dear." Belle studied the picture and sighed. "Such a shame. It truly was her crowning glory."

"It must have been awful for her. Not just the loss of hair, but the loss of, well, her identity."

Cleo ran her fingers through her own hair. It was fine as thistledown and exposure to the rain had left it more unmanageable than usual. No one in their right mind would call hair like hers a "crowning glory." She considered it the bane of her existence, which was why she kept it short. But when she imagined being without it, she shuddered and thought, So what if it's not perfect? It's part of me.

Yet there were parts of herself she had given up, memories she had chosen to ignore, huge chunks of the past she had tried to escape. She had severed family ties more essential to her identity than her hair, and she had cut herself off from the one person who might have understood.

Forgive me, Aunt Elspeth. I didn't know. . . .

She remembered the last time she saw her aunt. It had rained that day, too, the day of her mother's memorial service. She remembered the crowd outside the church, the circle of cameras, the crush of reporters, and Grandmother Dennis's rebuke.

"This is a funeral, gentlemen. Not a circus."

She recalled the ride to the cemetery, the sickening smell of flowers at the graveside, and Elspeth holding her hand. Her aunt hadn't said anything, though. Not then. But when the rituals were over and it was time for her to leave, she had asked Cleo to walk her to her car, and in their final moments together, she had said, "There are two kinds of people in this world, child. Those who curse ugliness and those who celebrate beauty."

"Is that anything like pessimists and optimists?" Cleo asked, more from politeness than interest.

"That's part of it, but only part." For a while Elspeth was silent, groping for a way to make Cleo understand. They were skirting a puddle in the driveway when all at once she stopped walking and pulled Cleo to a halt beside her.

"Look at that, child, and tell me what you see."

Mystified, Cleo stared from the puddle to her aunt. "I see a mud puddle, Aunt Elspeth."

133

"Anything else?"

"N-no," she answered. "Just a puddle."

Elspeth smiled and shook her head. "Look again, child. Keep on looking. Maybe some day you'll see a piece of the sky."

I looked, Aunt Elspeth, Cleo thought. I'm still looking. At least in that I haven't let you down.

She had learned to appreciate aesthetics in art, in her work, and in nature. But more often than not, the beauty in people eluded her. People were inconsistent. There were women like Grandmother Dennis, who had instructed her lawyer to file a restraining order against Elspeth Jarman.

"My granddaughter is all I have left in the world," she had said. "I don't want her influenced by that woman." And in practically the same breath, she'd scolded Cleo for tracking mud on the carpet.

There were women like Suzanne, who had told the world how much she loved her daughter, but never got around to telling Cleo.

And there were men like Joe, who were here today, gone tomorrow. To say he was fickle seemed an understatement. Last night he'd romanced her in the kitchen. Tonight he'd disappeared.

He wasn't in his room at ten thirty, when she said good night to Belle and went to bed, and although she lay awake, listening for his step on the stairs, at midnight he still hadn't returned.

The rain continued on Tuesday. When Cleo encountered Joe in the second floor hallway, she wished him a cool good morning and breezed past him toward the stairs. She would have given a week's income to know what he'd been up to the previous evening, but she didn't want Joe to know she'd been aware of his absence. She hoped someone else would ask him about it, and at breakfast Belle did.

"Cleo was looking all over for you last night," she said. "Where did you disappear to?"

"The basement," Joe said. "There are several storage rooms down there. I thought I'd check 'em out."

"Did you find anything?" asked Pete.

"No clue, if that's what you mean." The grin Joe gave Cleo told her he was happy she'd missed him. But by noon Joe's good humor had started to fade.

"It's this damn weather," he said. "It's not fit for human habitation."

"The rain's getting to everyone," said Cleo. After a glance at the far end of the parlor assured her Pete was busy reading *A Man With A Maid,* she took Joe's hand and drew him onto the love seat beside her. "I don't know if you've noticed," she whispered, "but Pete's stopped taking pictures and Tiffany hasn't combed her hair since breakfast and Andrew's hardly budged from that Hudson and Belle's stopped smiling."

"Go on. Rub it in."

"You're overreacting, Joe, but I'm sure it'd help if we found the clue."

"Tell me about it." Joe stifled a yawn and stretched out, his feet hanging over the arm of the love seat, his head in her lap. Another yawn overcame him as he said, "Why do you think I spent last night poking around the basement."

He looked boyish and appealing with his eyes shut, and he sounded so weary. Cleo wanted to comfort him, and since words seemed inadequate, she smoothed her fingers

135

along the worry lines on his forehead. But that seemed inadequate too.

She bent down to trace the lines on his brow with kisses and at the first touch of her lips, Joe rolled onto his side. Before she could protest, Joe sat up and wrapped his arm about her.

She was trying to wriggle away from him when his mouth found hers. His lips were sweet and rough and urgent, but just when she was aching for more, he leaned back against the cushions, resting his cheek on the top of her head.

For a full minute she stayed as he had positioned her, waiting for his next move. Nothing happened except that the crisp V of chest hair at the open collar of his shirt tickled her nose and his arm about her waist grew heavy with relaxation. It seemed one brief, tantalizing kiss was all he'd intended.

The rustling of pages from the other end of the room reminded her they were not alone, and she pushed onto one elbow and studied Joe suspiciously. His breathing was deep and even.

"Joe," she whispered, giving his shoulder a shake, "you're not falling asleep, are you?"

"Nope," he answered drowsily. "Just thinking."

"About what?"

"A way to keep the mob off my back till the rain lets up."

"Why don't you think with your eyes open?"

"What for? I do my best thinking with them shut." He turned his head slightly, so that his face was angled toward her breasts. The feathery touch of his lips sent shivers of anticipation through her as he said, "You should try it, Cleo. I'm already beginning to get ideas."

136

"Yes, I can tell you are."

With one expert tug, Joe unfastened the button at the waistband of her slacks. In the same deft movement, he lowered the zipper and slid his hand inside the fabric.

"Joe, you wouldn't—"

But he did.

"You *can't*—"

But he was.

Oh, God! Much more of this and she'd never be able to stop him.

"What about Pete?" she whispered breathlessly.

"Let 'im get his own girl."

She wove her fingers through his hair, and for one delicious moment held him closer. And then, with her last shred of willpower, she gave a sharp pull.

"What the devil!" Joe's eyes popped open, then narrowed to irate slits.

"Please, Joe. We mustn't."

"Okay, Cleo. If that's the way you want it."

"That's how it *has* to be."

Cleo sprang to her feet and stumbled toward the fireplace, keeping a watchful eye on Pete. Her hands shook as she straightened her clothes.

"I'm sorry, Joe."

"Not half as sorry as I am." After a last speculative look at her, Joe frowned into the fire. "Those are the breaks," he said ruefully. "If you're not interested, I guess I'll have to find another way to amuse myself."

A smile played about the corners of his mouth, then widened into a grin that made her distinctly uneasy. He was still smiling when she left the parlor, but it wasn't till evening, when everyone had gathered around the dinner table, that Joe announced he had a surprise for them.

137

"You found the clue," said Andrew.

"No, that's not it," Joe replied.

"Well, just the same it's lovely," Belle said brightly. "I simply adore surprises."

"I hope you'll like this one," said Joe.

"What is it?" asked Pete.

Joe shook his head. "If I told you, it wouldn't be a surprise."

"Can't you give us a hint?" said Belle.

"Yes," said Tiffany. "Just a tiny one."

"Nope. But if you come to the library after supper, I'll show you what it is."

Despite Belle's interrogation, Pete's badgering, and Tiffany's coaxing, Joe remained adamant. At nine o'clock, Cleo reported to the library, as much in the dark as her cousins.

Pete was the last to arrive. His face fell when he saw the semicircle of chairs around the television.

"Another videotape," he said disgustedly. "Big deal."

"This one's special," said Joe. "Sit down and have some popcorn."

He slid a cassette into the VCR, made some minute adjustments to the controls on the TV, and the heavy metal sounds of Roger Dennis's rock group filled the room.

A twinge of foreboding prompted Cleo to keep her distance from the rest of the party. She sank into a Windsor chair near the door just as the music reached a dissonant peak. The camera panned over the frenzied crowd at the concert, and the title of the film flashed on the screen.

"Rivals," Belle whispered. "Isn't that Suzanne's movie?"

Before she finished speaking the credits started to roll,

138

and Suzanne's name appeared in red letters, superimposed upon an extreme close-up of Roger Dennis.

For what might have been a minute the camera focused on his fingers, flying over the guitar strings, on the grinding movements of his shoulders and hips, on his feet stamping out the beat, and just when Cleo began to appreciate how talented a performer her father had been, the camera angle shifted, crazily, swiftly, tracking over blurred, adoring faces in the audience and finally returning to a freeze-frame of Roger's face.

His pose was familiar. Cleo had seen it on album covers and posters and in countless magazines. Head thrown back, mouth stretched wide, eyes closed, utterly transported by the music. And then the screen faded to black and the blare of rock music and the screams of her father's fans were replaced by the imperious shriek of a telephone.

A lamp clicked on, spotlighting the phone. Beyond this bleak, unnatural light, a nightstand and bureau and a sumptuous bed remained gray and shadowy, as did the woman who answered the call. Only Suzanne's hands were illuminated as she fumbled for the receiver, and her fingernails were long and painted a glamorous candy-apple red.

"Mrs. Dennis?"

"Yes, Captain Benicke."

"I'm afraid it's bad news, ma'am."

Suzanne whimpered and slumped forward, as if she could not support her burden of grief. The lamplight fell upon her pale shining hair, and as Captain Benicke informed her the Coast Guard had recovered her husband's body, she turned her tear-streaked face toward the camera.

In the hands of a competent actress, the scene that followed would have been effective, perhaps even touching. But Suzanne overplayed it. Her gestures were too broad, her expressions studied, her delivery melodramatic. And her grief seemed synthetic; a matter of smudged mascara and glycerin tears. Cleo didn't want to watch, yet she couldn't bear to look away. Her mother had had small roles in half a dozen films, but she had seen none of them. Till now.

If she were to walk out, wouldn't she be betraying Suzanne?

She wasn't sure, and so she sat near the library door and watched as the story unfolded, and gradually she recognized how flawed the movie was.

The cinematography was good, but the film had been poorly edited. Some scenes were too long, others cut too quickly. The premise was thin, the dialogue stilted, the relationships confusing, and the flashbacks a disaster. But Cleo discovered a certain fascination in watching a movie as bad as *Rivals*. She wondered what her cousins thought of it.

They were munching popcorn, and there was some shuffling of feet and a good deal of squirming about, but aside from that they were silent until fifteen minutes into the film, when the woman Roger had gotten involved with shortly before his death made her entrance. Through some mix-up in plans, she and Suzanne were seated in adjoining pews at Roger's funeral. After the services, Suzanne confronted her rival over her husband's open casket and said, "I have a bone to pick with you."

"Was that supposed to be a pun?" asked Belle.

She never took her eyes off the screen. Obviously, she intended her question to be taken seriously, but someone

140

—probably Pete—snickered, and the spell of embarrassment was broken.

From that point on the Jarmans seemed to find something comical in everything that happened on the screen. They ridiculed the soap opera twists of the plot and poked fun at Suzanne's acting, and although much of their criticism was valid, Cleo resented them making jokes at her mother's expense.

They were engaged in a lively debate, discussing whether *Rivals* was a bigger bomb than *Plan 9 From Outer Space,* when Cleo decided she'd had all she could take.

She left the library quietly and headed for the veranda, where the rain stopped her escape and the night air cooled her stinging cheeks. She was unaware Joe had followed her until he spoke.

"Why do you always run away?"

"Run away?" she echoed, her voice shrill with disbelief. "Let me tell you something, Joe Gamble. *Rivals* may be a bad joke to you, but it happens to be my life."

She tried to walk away from him, but his arms curved about her and held her prisoner.

"Look, honey, for whatever it's worth, tonight's the first time I saw the movie. I had no idea it was so bad, and my only motive for running it was to entertain your cousins, maybe give their morale a boost."

"Well, you certainly succeeded. They seem to think it's a laugh riot."

"That's not what I intended, Cleo, I swear. I recognized my mistake almost immediately."

"But you expected me to sit there and watch it."

"No. No, of course not. But as you said, it's part of your life." His voice was gentle, almost hesitant. But there was no hesitation in his hands on her shoulders, nor was there uncertainty in the way he turned her to face him.

"It *is* your life, Cleo," he went on soberly, with more conviction. "It's not of your making, and maybe it's not the kind of life you'd have chosen, but you can't escape it. Not indefinitely. Sooner or later, you've got to come to terms with it."

She stared at him, at a loss, her eyes stormy. "That's why I'm here, isn't it? That's the reason Aunt Elspeth arranged all this."

"Maybe partly." Joe sighed and shook his head. "I just don't know, Cleo."

"But you had your suspicions." She wished it weren't so dark, wished she could see him more clearly. "How long, Joe? Did you suspect the truth when you came to Mendocino?"

"What if I did?"

"Well, you might have *told* me."

Joe smiled and pressed her head to his shoulder, swaying from side to side. Bemused and more than a little exasperated, he said, "Would it have made a difference?"

Cleo did not reply, but her body acknowledged defeat. She felt herself weakening, clinging to Joe as she admitted that if he had leveled with her it would not have changed a thing. Without him, she felt incomplete. Her breath quickened at the sight of him and her heart sang because she loved him. She always had, she always would. Nothing could change that. Not years of separation or her aunt's schemes or her mother's movie or her own empty pride.

His lips were mere inches away from hers, and it was she who closed the gap. She kissed him shyly at first, and then with a fast-growing intensity that left both of them shaken. Their lips met again in a sensual assault, and this time there was no holding back.

She framed his face between her palms and explored his mouth with a voluptuous eagerness that promised passion and surrender. By the time the kiss ended, neither of them knew who was the victor and who the vanquished, and neither of them cared.

Joe slouched against a pillar and hauled her tight against him so that she could feel how much he wanted her. He felt the response that trembled through her and ached to touch her more intimately.

"God, Cleo," he groaned. "This kissing in corners is driving me crazy."

Tormented by the imprint of her breasts against his chest, he cradled her between his thighs and hugged her closer. He ran his hands over her hips, over the sweet roundness of her buttocks, then trailed questing fingertips along her thighs, again and again, venturing higher with each foray, until finally he was stroking the soft womanly warmth of her.

An inner alarm, so shrill that it seemed audible, warned Cleo to retreat before she crossed the threshold from temptation to seduction, and she gasped, "Not here, Joe. Now now."

"Why?" he countered thickly. "I like here and now, and I especially like you."

He wanted to take her now, this instant, here on the dark veranda, with the wind whipping around them and the surf crashing on the rocks below them and the rain falling in a silvery curtain that created the illusion of privacy. But he only kissed her once more and buried his face against the side of her neck. For a few moments longer he held her in his arms, and then he put her away from him.

She's still running, he thought. But someday she'll realize there are some things she can't run away from.

And when that day came, God willing, he'd be there.

CHAPTER ELEVEN

Cleo woke to blue skies and birdsong the next morning. When she walked into the kitchen, she was greeted by Belle, who was sliding a pan of popovers into the oven.

"Isn't it a gorgeous day?" the older woman caroled. "Now all we have to do is watch the shadows."

Over breakfast everyone agreed to separate into two groups, the men at the landing, the women on the terrace.

Joe said, "If we find the clue, we'll signal with the boat whistle. If you find it, give a blast on the air horn."

By eleven o'clock both parties were in place. Cleo and Belle made themselves comfortable in lawn chairs near the sundial, but Tiffany could not sit still. She wandered through the shrubbery and walked the rail fence and eventually found her way to the fountain.

"I *hate* waiting," she said. "I don't think I can make it till noon."

"Maybe you won't have to," said Belle. "You can see that the house shades most of the terrace."

"Yes, except for the sundial."

"Exactly. And the pattern isn't likely to change much in the next forty-five minutes."

"The shadows will recede," said Cleo.

Belle's jaw dropped. "Are you sure about that?"

"Positive, unless the sun takes a wrong turn and moves lower in the sky instead of higher."

"I was thinking they'd get longer," Belle murmured. "But no matter. If we put our heads together, we ought to be able to figure out where the shadows will fall at twelve o'clock."

"What if we do?" Tiffany demanded. "Joe couldn't find out how the clues were packaged, so we still don't know what we're looking for."

"That's the least of our worries," Belle replied brightly. "Just imagine you're Elspeth—"

"Not on your life," Tiffany muttered.

"Well, then, imagine you have something to hide."

"Yes, Tiffany," Cleo broke in, fed up with the girl's petulance. "That should be right up your alley."

"You ought to know," Tiffany shot back.

"Girls, *girls*!" Belle intervened. "Bickering won't solve anything."

"Neither will pouting," said Cleo.

Tiffany sucked in her lower lip and advanced on Cleo, hands on her hips. "Look who's talking. Rebecca of Sunnybrook Farm—"

"Tiffany, that's enough," Belle cautioned.

"Why are you picking on me? Cleo started this."

"And I'm finishing it," Belle declared.

"But—"

"Not another word, young lady."

After a venomous glance at Cleo, Tiffany flounced back to the fountain and sat on the edge, grudgingly obeying Belle's gag rule, but the way she scooped up a pebble and flung it into the water was openly defiant.

If Belle noticed this display she chose not to comment.

She patted a stray curl into place with the aplomb of a peacock smoothing ruffled feathers and said, "Now, where were we?"

"Pretending we have something to hide."

The splash of a second pebble striking the water punctuated Cleo's reply.

"Oh, yes," said Belle.

A louder splash.

If Belle can ignore Tiffany, so can I, thought Cleo. She lay back in her chair and turned her face toward the sun as Belle continued.

"If Elspeth's running true to form . . ."

Splash, splash.

". . . the clue is another poem. Which means it has to be in a weatherproof container. Something plastic or metal or glass."

Another splash, this one more restrained. Tiffany was leaning over the rim of the fountain, fishing for something in the water.

What on earth is she up to? Cleo wondered. She watched Tiffany from beneath her lashes as she suggested, "Like a jelly glass or a mayonnaise jar?"

"Could be," said Belle, "although it might be simpler to laminate it."

"But that wouldn't give it much weight."

"How about a test tube?" Tiffany called.

"That's a possibility," Belle allowed. "But how would you keep it watertight?"

"Easy. You'd double seal it with a rubber stopper and paraffin."

"Well, I guess that would work."

Tiffany was on her feet now, approaching them, and as

she stepped out of the shade the sun glinted on the small glass cylinder in her hand.

"Oh, my God! She's found the clue." Cleo barely breathed the words. She was halfway across the terrace before they were spoken, and she and Tiffany were giggling and hugging each other and whirling across the terrace in a gleeful jig before Belle could assimilate what had happened.

"Oh, my word!" Belle cried. She rose and tried to join the celebration, but her knees buckled. Cleo and Tiffany caught her, one at either elbow, before she sank to the ground.

"Are you all right?" Cleo asked as they helped her back to the lawn chair. "Can I get you anything? A glass of water?"

"No, dear. I'm fine. Never better. I got up too fast, that's all."

Tiffany was fanning Belle with her sun hat. "She's awfully pale."

"I'm fine," Belle insisted. "Just surprised. I mean, my gracious! After all our searching. What do we do now?"

"We should signal the men," said Cleo.

"Right," said Tiffany, holding up the test tube. "And then we open this sucker." She stayed with Belle while Cleo ran off to sound the alarm. Within minutes Joe, Andrew, and Pete came loping up the hill from the landing.

"Ta-dum!" Tiffany welcomed them, displaying her find.

"Oh, wow!" Pete shouted. "Scope it out."

Andrew threw his arms about his daughter and gave her a loud, congratulatory kiss, and Joe gave her a pat on the back and a hearty "Way to go, Tiff!"

148

"This is so excellent!" Pete looked at his sister with new respect, awed by her achievement.

"It most certainly is," said Andrew. "Tell us, honey, where'd you find it?"

"Glad you asked." Beaming at her father, Tiffany pointed toward the trio of trumpeter swans that graced the fountain and said, "Gentlemen, may I present the 'brazen band.'"

Recognition dawned as the men studied the sculpture. The swans had been captured in graceful flight, transecting the midday shadow of the weather vane.

"Of course," said Andrew. "It's perfectly logical."

"Once you know where it was hidden," Joe qualified.

"When can we see the clue?" asked Pete.

Tiffany laughed and ruffled her brother's hair. "How about now?"

"Now's good," he said.

Cleo and Belle had remained on the far side of the fountain, allowing Tiffany center stage, and after beckoning them to gather round she peeled off the wax coating at the lip of the test tube, removed the stopper, and dumped the contents into her hand.

"There seem to be two messages," she said as she smoothed out the scrolled paper. "This one says, 'Halleluia! You have found the first clue.'"

A spontaneous cheer went up from the rest of the party. When the hurrahs died down, Tiffany went on.

"'Since you have progressed this far you must be: one, very lucky; two, very clever; three, a great team player; or four, all of the above. I wish you continued good fortune in your quest for my treasure.'"

"Is that it?" asked Belle.

"That's it, except it's signed, Elspeth Jarman."

149

"Now the clue," Pete urged.

Tiffany unrolled the second piece of paper. "It's another poem," she said. "Or part of one. 'Over the dunes, beside the bay, the fisherman's hut will make your day.'"

"That's straightforward enough," said Andrew.

"Yeah," said Pete. "This one's a cinch."

As it turned out, he was right.

The six of them made the trek to the western tip of the island, planning their strategy as they went. They arrived at the cabin, and after two hours of searching, Belle found one of the blind packets the students had hidden beneath a loose floor board on the stoop. Less than five minutes later, Pete found another test tube taped to a rafter in the darkest reaches of the sleeping loft.

There were no encouraging notes in this test tube, however; only a scroll which read, "A tisket, a tasket, go find my little basket."

"This clue doesn't specify location," said Belle. Turning to Joe, she asked, "Where do we begin?"

"Here," Joe replied. "There's a stack of bushel baskets in the root cellar."

"What if we come up empty?" asked Pete.

"In that case I'd suggest we split into teams and search the buildings. You and your dad can take the carriage house, Belle and Tiffany the top two floors of the lodge, and Cleo and I will search the ground floor and basement. Whoever finds anything can signal the others with the air horn."

Although Cleo was anxious to get on with the hunt, she wasn't sure she wanted to be paired off with Joe. She wondered if she should question the makeup of the teams, but before she could raise the issue, her cousins had given Joe's proposal their unanimous approval.

I'm fresh out of options, she thought. If she made a fuss now, she'd look like a spoilsport, and besides, the message narrowed the search to baskets, so what could be easier? Someone would find the next clue in no time.

Cleo cast her lot with the others, believing she had considered all the angles. But her quick calculations overlooked the number of baskets there were on Chelsea, and their variety. There were big baskets and small ones, plain baskets and fancy ones, baskets made of wicker and willow and rattan, baskets molded from ceramics and plastic, baskets for every conceivable purpose. There were wastebaskets, breadbaskets, sewing and laundry baskets. And these were merely the tip of the iceberg.

Cleo grumbled as she followed Joe down the basement stairs. "I had no idea there were so many kinds of baskets."

"Careful," said Joe. "This banister's full of dry rot. And hang on to your hat, lady. You ain't seen nothin' yet."

"You mean there are more baskets down here?"

"Uh-huh. I found quite a few the other night."

At the foot of the stairs Joe turned to his right. He continued through the main room of the cellar, where the furnace crouched in a gloomy corner, past a laundry room and lavatory, and finally led Cleo into a dark, musty storeroom. A light bulb dangled by its cord from the ceiling, and when he turned it on Cleo jolted to a stop.

Finding one small basket among the mountain of cartons and barrels and trunks that filled the room would be like looking for a shamrock in acres of clover. Too stunned to move, she watched Joe wrestle one of the

151

boxes into the light, and for the first time, she appreciated the enormity of their undertaking.

"Didn't my aunt ever throw anything away?" she wailed.

Joe sat on his heels and glanced at her. She was leaning against the doorjamb like a flower drooping on its stem, and she looked as dispirited as she sounded.

"Listen, Cleo," he said, "it's almost six o'clock. We've been on the go since sunup. Would you like to take a break before we begin?"

"No," she answered grimly. "I can keep going if you can."

The challenge in her voice might have struck sparks, but it was impossible to take her seriously when she had a smudge of dust on her nose. Joe smiled and said, "It's not as bad as it seems, honey. I've already gone through most of this stuff."

"But there are other storage rooms."

"Yes. And the wine cellar."

Cleo inhaled deeply and stepped away from the door, rolling up her sleeves. "Let's get going," she said. "The sooner we get started, the sooner we'll be done."

Thirty minutes later, checking through a stack of strawberry baskets as long as her arm, she regretted her decision.

By seven o'clock she was contrite. They had finished with the storerooms and she was beginning to realize how much Joe's groundwork had streamlined this chore. "I'm sorry I've been such a crybaby," she said. "I don't know what got into me. Maybe I have a low frustration level."

"Or low blood sugar." Joe grinned at her over his shoulder. "You always did get cranky when you were hungry."

Cleo scowled. She had admitted her fault and apologized. The least Joe could've done was disagree with her.

She followed him into the wine cellar and barely gave him time to turn on the light before she slammed the door, and the next sound she heard was the rattle of metal on concrete as the doorknob popped off and skidded across the floor.

Joe started and swung around to face her. "What was that?"

"N-nothing," she faltered, crossing her fingers behind her back. If only he would go about his business, she might be able to replace the doorknob on its post.

Joe obviously didn't believe her. He cocked an eyebrow at her, but she held her ground by the door. She maintained a wide-eyed, innocent stare, and at last he shrugged and turned away. When he had disappeared into one of the brick archways that housed a forest of empty wine racks, she recovered the knob and made a hasty assessment of the damages. Working carefully, Cleo tried to repair the mechanism without making any noise that would arouse Joe's suspicions, but it soon became apparent that caution wasn't enough. She felt the post sliding away and tried to catch hold of it, but decades of wear and tear had stripped the grooves from the metal. Only a slick steel nubbin protruded from the escutcheon.

She dropped to her knees, holding onto the post for all she was worth, but the weight of the doorknob on the other side of the door pulled the post free of her grip. She heard the unmistakable sound of the knob hitting the floor outside, and sank down beside the door, horrified at what she'd done.

Why did I try to fix it? she wondered. And why did I

lie to Joe? But motives didn't matter. All she could do now was confess.

She got to her feet and brushed the dust off her skirt. She combed her hair with her hands, making herself as presentable as possible. It didn't do much for her confidence.

"Uh, Joe," she called.

"Find something?"

"N-no, it's just . . ." She paused to clear her throat. "We seem to have a problem."

"We do? What sort of problem?"

"I—well, it's the door."

There was a harsh exclamation, and then Joe came striding toward her. She moved to one side so that he could see what had happened for himself.

After a tense silence, he asked, "Where's the doorknob?"

"Right here," she said, placing it in his hand.

He gave her a quizzical frown. "Where's the rest of it?"

"On the other side of the door."

In the blink of an eye, his expression went from perplexed to forbidding. The oath he muttered made her wince.

"I, uh, I guess that means you can't fix it," she said.

"How the hell can I fix it when I don't have half the parts?"

"I thought maybe you could take the door off its hinges."

"Think again, Cleo. And while you're thinking, take another look at the door."

She did as he instructed. "Oh, of course. I see. The hinges are on the outside."

154

"Correct."

"Well, then, can't we maybe break it down?"

"You've gotta be kidding." Joe hammered the side of his fist against the wood. "Hear that? This thing is solid. The whole place is built like a fortress."

"Then how do we get out?"

"We don't. Not till someone comes looking for us."

"But that could take *hours*!"

"I doubt it. It's almost dinnertime—"

"Please, don't mention dinner." Cleo wrapped her arms about her middle. Suddenly, she was famished.

"The others will be hungry too," Joe said. "I don't think anyone else stopped for lunch."

"Did you?"

"I grabbed a sandwich and—hey! That reminds me. I have some cookies."

Cleo's eyes lit up. Her mouth watered at the thought of food, and she watched Joe's every move as he removed a cellophane packet from his shirt pocket. She was hoping for Oreos, or maybe chocolate chips, but when she got a closer look at the cookies, she wrinkled her nose with distaste.

"Fig Newtons," she said flatly.

Joe brushed lint off the wrapper and offered her the packet. "They're kind of crumpled, but they taste good. Have one."

"Maybe later," she replied. "I should've known a man who drowns his food with ketchup would have developed a taste for Fig Newtons." Joe looked decidedly grumpy as he shoved the cookies into his shirt pocket, and Cleo realized how ungracious she had sounded. "Thanks all the same," she said, "but I don't want to spoil my appetite for supper. I can wait till we're out of here."

* * *

At nine thirty they were still waiting. They'd heard footsteps crossing the floor above them once—at least, Cleo thought they were footsteps. Joe said it was wishful thinking.

"What's up there?" she'd asked.

"The music room."

"Then they must be looking for us."

"How do you figure that?"

"Why else would anyone be in there?"

Certain that rescue was imminent, she had pounded on the walls and shouted at the ceiling, but all she'd gotten for her troubles were sore hands and a hoarse throat.

Joe tried to bolster her spirits. He found a paddleball beneath one of the wine racks and challenged her to a match. Unfortunately, the rubber band broke almost immediately. The ball bounced across the floor and rolled behind a pile of packing crates, which led to Joe's next discovery.

He squeezed behind the crates to retrieve the ball, and while he was there he found a rollaway bed. He seemed inordinately pleased with himself as he trundled the cot to the center of the room and removed the tarpaulin that covered it.

Grinning at Cleo, he said, "How about that?"

She tested the mattress and replied, "This is great. Now we can starve in comfort."

"It's not as bad as all that," Joe argued. "Why don't you lie down for a while. You'll feel better if you get some sleep."

"No, thank you."

The thought of being trapped in the wine cellar overnight made her want to weep. And so, while Joe prowled

156

about the room, looking for another diversion, she sat on the edge of the cot, disconsolate, elbows on her knees, chin in her hands, counting the cracks in the cement floor.

In an effort to shake her out of her misery, Joe said, "You don't know when you're well off, Cleo."

"How kind of you to share that insight with me." Her tone of voice made it plain that she didn't think he was being kind at all. But she knew he was right.

The situation could be a lot worse. They could've been locked in one of the cramped, airless storerooms. The wine cellar might not be palatial, but it was large enough that they wouldn't get claustrophobic. And for the sake of the wine, it was vented. The fresh salt air pervaded the room and carried the tangy scent of the sea. If she closed her eyes, Cleo could almost convince herself she was running across the sand, racing the waves at Treasure Bay. If she concentrated very hard, she could imagine the feel of the wind in her hair.

But I'm not on the beach, she thought fiercely. I'm alone in the wine cellar with Joe.

At this disturbing reminder, she wondered if there was any possibility Joe had arranged this. He'd had the opportunity Monday night, and if the way he'd been coming on to her was any indication, he'd also had the motive.

But *I* slammed the door, Cleo thought. Joe couldn't have planned that.

Or could he?

He knew her well. Sometimes it seemed he knew her better than she knew herself, and he had an incredible knack for pushing just the right buttons to ignite her temper or evoke tenderness or arouse passion.

A few minutes later, when Joe returned from his expedition to the hinterlands of the cellar, she was digging at one of the wider cracks in the floor with the toe of her sandal, trying to decide whether their confinement was accidental or deliberate.

"Things are looking up," he said.

But Cleo wasn't. She kept digging at the crack. She didn't even glance at him as she inquired, "What did you find this time? A secret passageway?"

"Nope. Something better."

To prove his point, Joe held a bottle of vintage cabernet under her nose, and she reacted with a listless, "How will you open it?"

Joe grinned, and through some skillful sleight of hand, produced his penknife from behind her left ear.

"That's quite a trick," she said.

"Wait'll you see the encore."

He opened the penknife and began carving out slivers of cork with the blade, and she sat up a bit straighter, watching him, captivated by the play of muscle and sinew in his big, sun-browned hands.

"I am kind of thirsty," she admitted.

"So am I."

She moistened her lips and moved closer. "I thought the wine racks were empty."

"Most of them are. We drank the last of the Beaujolais the night we came. But there's some Bordeaux toward the back of the cellar and a few bottles of champagne." As he spoke, Joe embedded the end of the blade in the last chunk of cork and eased it out of the bottle. "See how easy it is when you know what you're doing," he said.

Cleo applauded, and he bowed from the waist as he handed her the wine.

"Just a second," he cautioned. "Don't drink it yet."

He made another trip to the back of the cellar, and this time he returned carrying the stub of a candle and a box of wooden matches.

"You're prepared for everything," she remarked.

"I try," he allowed modestly.

It was true, she realized. He did try. He had been sweet and attentive all evening, and she felt like a rat for mistrusting him, but she couldn't help feeling uneasy as he propped the lit candle in a pool of melted wax on the floor and turned off the overhead light. Even the cot conspired against her. The mattress dipped beneath Joe's weight as he sat beside her, propelling her toward him until the hard length of his thigh stopped her slide.

She sprang to her feet and turned the light back on. "It's awfully dark without it," she explained.

"Yes, it is, but after your crack about the ketchup, I wanted to show you what a classy guy I can be." Joe slanted a grin at her and tossed the packet of Fig Newtons on the mattress. "Voila, ma'amselle. Dinner is served."

He's trying to entertain me, she thought. What could be more innocent?

She didn't turn the light off, but she managed a smile as she reclaimed her seat on the cot, and she took one of the cookies. "Now can I drink?" she asked.

"Please do."

She took a swig of cabernet and passed the bottle to Joe. He ate one of the Fig Newtons, washed it down with wine, and passed the bottle back. Following his example, she took a bite of cookie and chased it with cabernet. The clash of flavors made her shudder.

"*Yuck*. That's awful!"

Joe wolfed down another Fig Newton and reached for the bottle. "It's an acquired taste. Try again."

She complied with his advice, and after a few more bites of cookie and as many swallows of wine, she said, "You know, this isn't half bad." After another taste or two, she conceded, "In fact, it's pretty good."

Joe laughed and said he'd told her so.

On further reflection, Cleo decided it was more likely that the wine had numbed her taste buds, but her other senses had never been more acute. She was keenly aware of Joe. She heard the rumble of laughter from deep in his chest, and when his laughter abated, she heard his even breathing. She seemed to see his least gesture in slow motion. Watching his fingers caress the glassy curve of the bottle, she imagined he was caressing her. She saw the bunching of his biceps as he raised the bottle to his mouth, and she recalled how strong his arms had felt about her. She saw the way his throat worked as he swallowed, and she had a sudden wild impulse to lay her cheek against his chest. She wanted to feel his warmth and listen to the cadence of his heart and inhale the sea-breeze fragrance of his skin. . . .

Cleo realized Joe was staring at her as intently as she was studying him and belatedly glanced away. The next time he offered her the bottle, she waved it aside.

"Had enough?" he drawled.

"Too much."

The wine had gone to her head, or maybe she was drunk with her imaginings. Whatever the cause, she felt unreal and slightly woozy. When Joe set the bottle on the

160

floor and reached for her, her equilibrium became even more tenuous. He was solid and strong, her anchor to stability. Without him, she might drift away, and so she let him put his arm around her and nuzzle the side of her neck.

"Know what I'd like to do?" He cupped her chin in his hand, exerting a steady pressure that tipped her face toward his. "I'd like to pour cabernet all over your body."

"And then?" she prompted in a breathless whisper.

"Well, then I'd like to lick it off."

Everything womanly in her seemed to liquefy, to melt and yearn for him. But some fragment of caution tempered her response. She aligned her forearm with his, comparing her cameo-fair skin with his swarthiness.

"That's an interesting idea, Joe, but your coloring's much better suited to red wine than mine is."

Joe's eyes glinted with mock alarm. "I realize you tend to be a purist, Cleo, but don't tell me you go along with the rules about color coding wine to food."

"Yes. I happen to believe colors contribute flavors all their own."

"Where'd you get an idea like that?"

"From personal experience. Take chili peppers, for instance. Haven't you ever thought how strange it is that anything green should taste so hot?"

Joe's grin was positively wolfish as he raised her hand to his lips and pressed a kiss into her palm. "Seems to me you just shot your theory down."

"Well, maybe chilis aren't the best example, but think about it, Joe. Think how many colors derive their names from food. There's burgundy and mustard, orange and chocolate, lime green, tomato red, lemon yellow—"

"Honey," Joe whispered, circling her wrist with a

161

bracelet of sweet, biting kisses. "Peaches and cream," he growled as he nibbled his way to her elbow.

Surprise kept Cleo speechless while he lingered at the bend of her arm. She felt the delicious swirl of his tongue, and by the time he transferred his attentions to her shoulder, she was too entranced to stop him. His lips roved over the pulse at the base of her throat again and again.

"Coconut," he decided at last, "with just a hint of almond."

He brushed a gentle kiss at the corner of her mouth. "Strawberries," he declared. He kissed her again, less gently, and Cleo began making her own taste tests. She kissed his eyelids, his forehead, the point of his chin. "Nectarines," she murmured. "Pomegranates. Bananas."

She kissed the bridge of his nose and the angle of his jaw, and then she returned to his mouth. She molded her lips to his as if she were starving for the taste of him, then deepened her explorations with quick darting movements of her tongue, and when she withdrew, her face was flushed and her eyes were lambent with desire.

Joe's breathing was ragged. His hands were rough with urgency as they moved over her back. But after one look at each other, they burst out laughing.

"I'll go along with the pomegranates," he teased, "but don't you think bananas are sort of obvious?"

"Perhaps, but you made me sound like a fruit cup."

Joe shook his head. "I thought I was being creative."

"So did I."

"Then you admit your color theory's so much hokum!"

"I admit I made it up, but I'm not sure it's hokum. This was not what you'd call a scientific test."

"Want to try it again with the lights off?" Cleo blushed

and looked away, and Joe smiled to himself and added, "If you don't want to do that, we could always go back to my original suggestion."

"About the cabernet?"

"Yes. Unless you have a serious hang-up about red wine versus white. If you do, I could break out some champagne."

She stared at him, her defenses crumbling. "Or I could pour the cabernet on you," she said.

Joe's arms closed around her before the words were out. He traced the contours of her mouth with his thumb, his eyes dark with wonder. "Cleo?" he whispered hoarsely. "My God, I can't believe it. Maybe I should bar the door."

"To keep Pete out?"

"To keep you in."

"You don't need to, Joe." She smiled and kissed him on the mouth. "This time I'm not running away." Her voice was soft, but her lips were softer. His arms tightened about her until he was holding her painfully, gloriously close, and suddenly, neither of them was teasing.

They kissed each other joyfully, playfully, until consumed by passion, they tumbled across the mattress in a wild tangle of limbs. Joe's hands were hot with eagerness as he caressed her through her clothes; her hands were cool, yet he caught fire wherever she touched him. Only minutes ago the night had seemed too long, the hours stretching endlessly toward morning. But with her in his arms, the hours seemed to telescope, to rush in upon themselves. He wished he had the power to stop time, to make it stand still so that he could savor each moment they were together, to savor her.

He whispered her name and told her she was beautiful.

He marveled at her softness, at the silken texture of her skin. It seemed imperative that he convince her how irresistible she was, how desperately he wanted her. He undressed her slowly, almost reverently, adoring her with his eyes, charting each curve, each sleek velvety hollow with kisses, learning the secrets of her body with a lusty thoroughness that left none of her unexplored, and she blossomed and ripened beneath his touch, beneath his hot seeking mouth, responding to his lovemaking with a delicate eroticism that spurred him to greater intimacies. And each intimacy was a revelation.

She undressed him with an awkward haste that spoke of innocence, but the delight she found in him more than compensated for her lack of experience. She caressed him eagerly, reveling in the proud angular beauty of bone and sinew and tightly knit muscle and smooth supple skin, and when he moved over her and entered her, she welcomed the demanding thrusts that brought them together with an abandon that bordered on rapture. Possessed by him, encompassing him, she felt as if her whole life and everything she had experienced were only a prelude to this moment; as if she had been created for Joe, to give him pleasure, to find fulfillment in him. She could scarcely contain her joy. She wanted to share her discovery with him, but all she could manage were inarticulate groans of pleasure.

She didn't think it was possible to feel more ecstatic, but when release came, she was stunned by its intensity, and as the delicious spasms faded, she felt revitalized, as if she had been reborn; lighter than air, yet too contented to move. She loved Joe so fervently, she thought she might burst with it, yet she felt utterly drained. She wanted to laugh. She wanted to weep. But all she could do was cling to Joe and cry his name.

"Hold me, Joe. Hold me."

"I will, honey. Always."

He pulled the tarpaulin over her and smoothed the damp tendrils of hair away from her brow, scattering kisses across her face. "I used to think if I had one night with you, I'd die a happy man," he said.

"And now?" she murmured.

He rubbed his cheek against hers, wondering how he could measure a need that had no limits, and although he didn't answer, the tenderness in his eyes expressed his feelings. She felt close to him, closer than she had ever felt to anyone. She was secure in his arms, sheltered by the protective curve of his body. Long after he had dozed off, she lay awake, aware of her vulnerability.

It was frightening to love anyone as much as she loved Joe. It was especially dangerous considering that he was very much *of* the world, a live-for-today, let-tomorrow-take-care-of-itself kind of man. To her, *always* meant forever; to Joe, she suspected, *always* meant "till someone more exciting comes along." He was involved with people in their infinite variety. He thrived on closeness. She was a hostage to the past, a loner who kept her distance. She had told herself she didn't need anybody, and she'd believed it. Perhaps her defenses had kept her a prisoner, but they had also kept her safe. She had never considered relinquishing them.

Until tonight.

It seemed ironic that she had surrendered to Joe while they were locked in the wine cellar, and she couldn't help wondering if she had traded one prison for another. But on further reflection she decided, if she could turn back the clock, she would not change a thing.

Loving Joe, making love with him was a risk she'd had to take. Honesty compelled her to admit she had no regrets. She smiled dreamily. Well, maybe one, she thought. She snuggled close to Joe, thinking the cabernet.

CHAPTER TWELVE

They heard the blast of the air horn at eight o'clock the next morning.

"Somebody found the clue," said Joe.

Cleo tried not to yawn. It was difficult to work up excitement for the treasure hunt when she was beginning to feel like a mushroom.

Over the next twenty minutes the signal was repeated several times, and her spirits rose a little with each blast. They heard footsteps from the music room and voices calling from somewhere outside the house.

"Good," Joe said. "They know we're missing. Maybe now we'll see some action."

But another half hour passed before they heard the clatter of someone running down the basement stairs. They heard muffled scraping sounds, and Pete's voice raised in conversation with someone in the kitchen.

"Over here," Joe shouted, pounding at the door, and seconds later a knock from outside answered his summons.

"Joe?" Pete called.

"I'm here, buddy. Cleo, too. Can you let us out?"

"I'd like to, but there's no knob on this door."

"Look on the floor. It must be there."

"Got it."

Within minutes, the doorknob was reassembled and they were free.

"Good job, buddy."

Joe thumped Pete on the back, and Cleo kissed his cheek. "I've never been so happy to see anyone," she said. Pete blushed and stammered and shuffled his feet, and finally recalled that he had completed only part of his mission. "I better let the others know you're okay," he said, taking the stairs two at a time.

Joe hurried after him, but Cleo stopped for a last look at the wine cellar before she headed toward the stairs. Sunlight spilled through the narrow, ground-level windows, picking out the ruddy hues in the brick archways and the ruby red sparkle of the cabernet. If one ignored the packing crates and the drifts of excelsior in the corners, the room had a certain rustic charm, especially now that the door was open. But she could understand Joe's brusque departure. His relief that they'd been rescued was natural. She herself was looking forward to a shower, a change of clothes, a cup of coffee, and most of all, an enormous breakfast.

But hadn't Joe been a bit too eager to make his getaway?

By the clear light of morning it seemed that last night's interlude was an aberration; a temporary insanity that was beautiful while it lasted. But now it was over. The sooner she accepted that, the better off she'd be.

Sentiment is a luxury you can't afford, she told herself. Don't expect declarations of undying love. Things like that only happen in fantasies. She took the bottle of cabernet with her when she left the basement, but only because it seemed a shame to waste half a liter of vintage wine.

In fact, the more she thought about it, the wiser it seemed to forget about last night; just put it out of her mind and behave as if nothing extraordinary had happened. She knew this would be difficult, knew it wouldn't be easy to regain the status quo, but she didn't realize it would be well nigh impossible until she walked into the kitchen and found Joe seated at the breakfast table, flanked by Belle and Tiffany.

She was prepared for him to treat her impersonally; instead he pulled out her chair and poured her coffee and gave her a kiss that made her toes curl and her pulse quicken.

She hadn't recovered from that surprise when Belle and Tiffany sprang the next one.

"You poor dear," Belle chirped as she passed Cleo the platter of scrambled eggs. "It must've been a frightful ordeal for you, spending the night in the cellar."

Cleo buttered an English muffin and let Joe field that one.

"It wasn't so bad," he said. "We had each other."

"I imagine that was a great comfort," Belle allowed, "but all the same, you must be exhausted."

"They don't look exhausted," Tiffany remarked, studying them over the rim of her coffee cup. She zeroed in on Cleo and added, "You should wear pink more often. It suits you."

"Yes, it does," Belle agreed. "I've never seen Cleo more radiant. Have you, Joe?"

"Maybe once or twice," he said. "But then, I've always thought she's special."

Cleo fidgeted with the dusky-rose collar of her blouse

and felt as if her face had been dyed to match. She didn't look at Joe, but she could feel him gloating.

"So tell us," Tiffany said, "what did you do to amuse yourselves all night?"

Cleo choked on her orange juice, and Joe handed her a napkin. "We talked," he said. "Drank a little wine, played a little paddleball . . ."

"Is that anything like racketball?" Belle asked.

"No," Tiffany answered. "It isn't."

"Well, what's the difference?"

"I'll explain later." Tiffany's expression was a model of amused tolerance. Her smile seemed to say "What else can you expect from a seventy-year-old ingenue?" But just when Cleo began to hope her cousins would stop encouraging Joe, Tiffany asked, "Who won?"

"We both did," he replied smoothly.

A kick in the shin interrupted Joe's recap of their night together. Since Cleo was wearing sandals, she suspected she'd done more damage to her toes than she had to his leg, but shutting him up was worth the pain. She added her own recap seamlessly, so that neither Belle nor Tiffany noticed the change of subjects.

"We never thought we'd be stuck there all night," she said. "We thought one of you would find us long before morning."

"We would have," Belle said, "if we hadn't had such a full day. It was after seven before Andrew and Peter finished searching the outbuildings. They helped Tiffany and me finish up in the attic, but by the time we were done it was late, and we were tired. We had a snack and went to bed, and I guess we all assumed you'd already gone to your rooms."

Belle smiled apologetically, and Tiffany picked up the

170

narrative. "And then this morning we found the clue, and when you didn't respond to the signal, we compared notes and it dawned on us that none of us had seen you since yesterday afternoon, and, well, you know the rest."

"Maybe Joe does, but I don't," said Cleo. "Tell me about the clue."

Tiffany set her coffee cup in its saucer. "You mean you haven't heard?"

"Gracious!" said Belle. "I thought Pete would fill you in immediately."

"He did me," said Joe. "Cleo must've missed it."

Belle started to say something, but Tiffany pleaded, "Let me tell her." Without waiting for the older woman's approval, she rushed on. "Daddy's insomnia kicked up last night. He said every time he closed his eyes, he saw baskets. Truckloads of them. Tons of them."

Cleo smiled and said she knew exactly how he'd felt.

"So when he fell asleep," Tiffany continued, "he had all these dreams about baskets. He was slam-dunking basketballs and sitting in the gondola of a hot air balloon. He was racing in the Tour de France, only he didn't have a bike. All he had was the basket. And then he was a snake charmer—"

"I get the general idea," Cleo said.

"Anyway, in his last dream, he was fishing, and when he woke up he knew where Elspeth had hidden the clue."

"Where was that?"

"In this old fishing creel in the boathouse. Daddy saw it yesterday morning, but he didn't think of it as a basket —at least, not consciously. Not till the solution came to him in a dream. Isn't that weird?"

"That sort of phenomenon isn't uncommon," Belle said. "My very own mother foresaw all kinds of events in

171

her dreams, including me. One night she dreamed she was shaped like a pear, and sure enough, a few weeks later, she found out I was on the way."

Cleo made a polite, noncommittal reply, then helped herself to the last of the scrambled eggs and said, "I gather you went ahead and opened the clue."

Joe nodded. "Andy and Pete are hot on the trail of the next one."

Belle glanced at the wall clock. "I wonder what's keeping them. I thought they'd find it in no time." She removed a scrap of paper from her apron pocket and pushed it across the table to Cleo. "You can see for yourself, this one's the easiest of all," she said, but before Cleo could read the clue, Belle recited it aloud: " 'My heart is like a crescent moon, waiting to be filled. My passion is a loving cup, waiting to be spilled.' "

"It does seem easy," Cleo murmured.

"It's open and shut," said Tiffany. "Especially with a case full of trophies in the carriage house."

Cleo looked from the notepaper to her cousins. "But this loving cup isn't in the trophy case. Not if it's the prize Aunt Elspeth won in the Harvest Moon Dance Contest."

Joe clapped the heel of his palm against his forehead. "My God, that's right! There's an article about the contest in one of Elspeth's scrapbooks."

"Do you know where she kept the prize?" asked Tiffany.

"It used to be in her bedroom," Cleo said. "She used it as a doorstop."

Belle and Tiffany rose as if they were puppets controlled by the same string. "I'll tell Daddy and Pete," Tiffany said.

172

"And I'll get the loving cup from Elspeth's room," said Belle. "We can meet back here in ten minutes."

The moment they left the kitchen, Cleo turned to Joe and demanded, "How could you?"

"Excuse me?"

He looked genuinely startled, but Cleo wasn't taken in. " 'We had each other,' " she mimicked. " 'Played a little paddleball.' "

"So *that's* why you kicked me."

Joe's easy grin irritated her all the more. She scowled at him and stood up, but before she could walk away, he pulled her onto his lap. "I didn't mean to upset you, honey. After last night, you must know that."

He sounded sincere, and somewhat mollified, she stopped struggling to escape. "I'd like to believe you, Joe."

"Try me, Cleo." With feathery kisses on her cheek, he coaxed her to look at him. "What did I say that was so wrong?"

"It's not so much *what* you said."

"No?"

"What bothers me is the way you said it. It's as if you were *boasting*. And your attitude—well, you couldn't have made it more abundantly clear that we slept together if you'd taken a full page ad in the newspaper."

"Cleo, sweetheart, I love you. I don't give a damn who knows it. I'm not ashamed we made love, and I refuse to act as if I am. If that conflicts with your need for privacy, we've got a problem, but it's nothing we can't work out. Not if we're willing to compromise. And I am. Are you?"

Her anger spent, Cleo kissed him on the mouth, her lips tender as a sigh.

She did want to resolve their differences. She couldn't

173

begin to tell him how much, and so she didn't try. She wanted to trust him, too, but wanting something was no guarantee she'd get it. Particularly where love was concerned.

The next two days passed in a flurry of activity. The night passed in Joe's embrace, in the excitement of his lovemaking. Then the weekend was upon them and Cleo realized that time was running out. Their ten days were almost over.

Shortly after noon on Saturday, they found the last clue. "This one's for the treasure," Joe declared when he had opened the test tube which had been disguised as a hummingbird feeder in the arbor. An enclosed note from Elspeth congratulated them on their perseverance.

Cleo and her cousins gave Joe their undivided attention as he read the message: " 'A granite angel guards the grave. Dust shrouds flesh and bone. How sad to spend eternity 'neath cumbrous wings of stone.' "

"The Mary Angelus monument," said Cleo.

"That's right," Joe replied soberly.

"We should have guessed," she murmured. "It overlooks Treasure Bay."

Pete and Tiffany had stopped listening. They were racing across the lawn toward the golf carts, and Andrew and Belle were not far behind.

"What are we waiting for?" Joe said, and grabbed Cleo's hand. Then they were running too, but in the opposite direction, making a beeline for the Coast Guard station at the northwest tip of the island.

Is this the end of our teamwork? Cleo wondered as she sprinted after him along the ridge trail. If one or all of her cousins had decided to go it alone, it was a toss-up who would find the treasure first. Her cousins had the advantage of speed, but driving the golf carts meant they would have to stick to the shoreline, which gave Joe and her the advantage in distance.

They plowed through the underbrush, cut through a pine grove, crossed gullies and climbed hills, until Cleo's legs felt rubbery and the brassy taste of fatigue filled her mouth. Her hand was numb from Joe's grip. She knew he must be as winded as she was, but he didn't stop for a breather. He dragged her after him as they plunged along the dry creek bed that led to the bluffs.

We'll give them a run for their money, she thought. And if they didn't win the race and her cousins chose not to share the treasure, she would survive the disappointment.

But what if Joe got to the treasure first? What if he chose not to divide it? Perhaps it wouldn't come to that. After all, Joe had her to slow him down. Perhaps by the time they reached the monument, her cousins would already have arrived, and she'd never have to find out whether Joe would keep the treasure.

Please, God, let the Jarmans find it, she prayed. But deep inside, she knew it was hopeless long before they broke into the clearing at the edge of the bluffs.

From that vantage point, she could see the monument, the ruined lighthouse, and the steep winding lane that gave access to the beach at Treasure Bay. There was no sign of her cousins.

The bluffs were deserted, the lane empty, but still Joe didn't stop. He maintained his breakneck pace, towing her relentlessly after him across the clearing to the very rim of the bluff. When he finally stopped running and let go of her hand, her knees buckled and she sank to the ground, her last ounce of energy gone.

Joe doubled over and braced his hands against his knees. She could hear his labored breathing above the violent thudding of her own heart, but they scarcely had time to recover before the golf carts came into view.

"There they are," Joe said.

Instead of making a dash for the monument, he slouched down next to Cleo to watch the carts chasing each other along the beach.

"What about the treasure?" she said.

Joe raised his eyebrows. "I'd rather wait for the others. Wouldn't you?"

Cleo smiled. "Yes," she answered happily. "I would."

A few minutes later her cousins arrived.

"What took you so long?" Joe asked.

"We went back to the arbor to look for you," Andrew replied.

After the long week of searching, it seemed appropriate to Cleo that the six of them approached the monument as a group. But for some reason, it seemed anticlimactic when they found a metal cashbox secreted beneath a loose stone at the base of the statue.

"Cleo," Joe said, handing her the cashbox. "Would you do the honors?"

She sat on the ground near the monument, holding the box on her lap, while the others stood around her.

Exposure to the elements had stiffened the stainless steel latches that sealed the lid of the box, and she worked them with difficulty, fumbling a bit with excitement. It seemed to take forever before the latches would move, but no one said anything. Only the cries of the gulls and the rhythmic wash of the breakers disturbed the silence.

And then the box was open and everyone stepped closer. Inside, Cleo found a second videotape, a loose-leaf notebook, a cassette recording with her name on it, and a small brass key. She handed the key to Joe.

"Looks like a safe-deposit box key," he said after a cursory inspection.

Belle was paging through the notebook. "These are some of Elspeth's poems."

Andrew took charge of the videotape. "Let's go back to the house and see what Elspeth has to say on this one," he suggested.

Oddly subdued, the group made its way back to the lodge, and by tacit agreement, gathered in the library. Even Pete and Tiffany seemed restrained.

While Joe set up the VCR, Cleo studied her cousins, thinking how much they had changed in the week she had known them. And surprised by the affection she felt, she wondered whether the greatest change was in her.

On the videotape, Elspeth thanked the Jarman's for visiting Chelsea and explained that there was sufficient cash in her safe-deposit box to cover their travel expenses. "Joe cosigned the forms at my bank," she said. "He'll see that you're reimbursed." She also expressed the hope that each of them would select a personal memento to take home.

After dinner that evening, they adjourned to the parlor, and over dessert, Cleo's cousins announced their selections.

"If you have no objection," Belle said to Cleo, "I'd dearly love to have those old photographs we were looking through the other evening."

"Consider them yours," Cleo replied.

"Thank you, dear." Belle beamed.

"How about you, Andy?" asked Joe.

"My choice won't come as a shock to anyone. I've decided to take the Hudson."

"It'll cost a pretty penny to ship it back to Ohio," Belle warned.

"I don't care if it costs more than it's worth," Andrew said. "It reminds me of the car my father used to drive."

"That's cool, Dad," said Pete. "Kinda like tradition. And speaking of tradition, I'd like to have some of Elspeth's books."

"You mean the poetry she published?" Andrew inquired.

"No, I mean part of her library."

"Which part?"

"Oh, you know. *Fanny Hill, The Lustful Turk*—"

"No can do," Andrew exclaimed, shaking his head. "Sorry, son, but your mother would skin us both."

Pete made a face, but after some argument he bowed to defeat and settled for the VCR.

"Wise decision," said Andrew. "Okay, Tiffany. Your turn."

Tiffany fingered the ropes of jet and turquoise beads that were belted around her waist and replied, "My choice won't surprise anyone either."

"You're taking Elspeth's shimmy dresses," said Cleo.

Tiffany giggled, completely abandoning her blasé pose. "My friends will just *die* when they see them."

Because Andrew planned to catch the seven A.M. ferry to the mainland the next day, the party had agreed to an early night, but before they went to their rooms Joe requested they take part in one last ritual.

178

He asked Cleo to see that everyone had a champagne goblet, and while she distributed the glasses, Joe produced the bottle of champagne he'd chilled. When he had served the wine, they formed a semicircle in front of the fireplace and raised their glasses high.

"To Elspeth," Joe said.

"To Elspeth," everyone chorused.

And when they had drunk the toast, they hurled their glasses into the fireplace, where they splintered into a thousand glittering shards.

"What a waste of lovely crystal," Belle murmured as she left the room.

"What a waste of champagne," said Tiffany.

"Seems extravagant on both counts," Andrew agreed after totaling up the value of the glasses and the wine.

"Everybody's a critic," Joe muttered.

"Not me," said Pete. "I just wish I had film for my camera."

"How about you?" Joe asked Cleo as they followed the others up the stairs. "Do you think my gesture was extravagant."

"Yes, I do," she said. "Extravagant and romantic. But never mind—Aunt Elspeth would've loved it."

CHAPTER THIRTEEN

The Jarmans were gone with the tide on Sunday morning, leaving Joe and Cleo to await the arrival of the historical society representative.

"This is it, Cleo," Joe remarked as they climbed the hill from the landing. "Today we hand over the keys. It's the end of an era, the changing of the guard—"

"I'd rather not think about it," Cleo broke in.

Now that they were alone, she had hoped Joe would talk about something other than Chelsea or her aunt or her cousins. Something more personal. His definition of *always,* for instance. Or his feelings for her. Or whether she would ever see him again.

"The party's over," she said as Joe opened the door to the lodge. "I have to finish packing."

"That makes two of us," Joe replied. "Have you chosen your memento yet?"

Cleo nodded, but she didn't tell him what she had selected. "Have you?" she asked.

"Uh-huh. Elspeth's record collection."

"It'll take a while to pack all those albums."

"Maybe. I don't know. Shouldn't be too bad." Joe consulted his watch. "Tell you what. Why don't we meet in the parlor in half an hour. We'll play Elspeth's tape and have a private celebration."

Cleo smiled. "Make it forty-five minutes and you're on." The prospect of a private celebration with Joe made the task that awaited her seem less dismal.

She needed no reminders of Chelsea. Her memories of her aunt would last a lifetime. But late last night, lying wakeful after Joe had fallen asleep, she had decided to keep a few souvenirs: the videocassette of her mother's movie, Elspeth's poetry, and some of her scrapbooks. This assortment of paper and film chronicled events that, until recently, had seemed overwhelming. Yet they fit into a single mover's carton.

And not a very big one, Cleo thought as she sealed the top of the carton with tape. If she could confront these things, pack them away, and carry the box downstairs, shouldn't she be capable of putting the past behind her?

She heard Joe picking out a tune on the piano when she left the box with her luggage in the foyer, and she returned to her room to wash her hands, run a comb through her hair, and freshen her lipstick before she ran downstairs to the parlor. She met Joe in the downstairs hall.

"Finished already?" he inquired.

He was holding a rolled page of sheet music in one hand, and she glanced at it curiously as she replied, "My packing didn't take as long as I thought it would."

"Good." He slapped the rolled paper against his palm. "Maybe later you'll help me out."

"I'll help right now if you'd like."

"But the tape—"

"Will wait a few minutes more," she finished. "Just tell me what you want me to do."

"That's a tall order, Cleo." Joe grinned and guided her into the parlor. When they were settled on the love seat, he unfurled the sheet music and handed it to her. "For openers, tell me what you make of this."

"It's a song by Cole Porter," Cleo said. "Is this what you were playing earlier?"

"Yes, but take a closer look."

Cleo did. " 'The Girl From the Second Act,' " she read. "The title sounds sort of twenties, but I don't think I've ever heard of it."

"That's because it's never been published." Joe tapped one finger against the top corner of the paper and said, "This is the original manuscript."

"Well, that's very interesting." Cleo offered the manuscript to Joe, but he pushed it back at her.

"You're not through yet," he said.

"I'm not?"

"Nope. Keep going."

Cleo knitted her brows and bent over the sheet. "What am I supposed to be looking for?"

"Just keep reading. You'll see."

She might have questioned his highhanded tactics, but his enthusiasm convinced her to follow directions, and she scanned the lyrics silently.

Some say she's Irish; some say French.
I say that's so much fiction.
She's an angel, a vixen, a lady, a tramp,
a red-haired bundle of contradiction.
Every night at the Follies,
and after the matinee,
the stage-door Johnnies gather,
and this is what they say:

I sent her flowers; she stole my heart.
She led me a merry chase from the start.
I was playing for keeps; she was playing a part.
But there's one delightful fact.
She's the girl from the second act.

Cleo finished reading and glanced at Joe. He was watching her impatiently, drumming his fingers on his thigh.

"Well?" he said.

"It reminds me of Aunt Elspeth. Were the lyrics composed for her?"

He tapped the corner of the paper again. "Look at that. Tell me what it says."

" 'Music by Cole Porter, lyrics by'—my God, Joe! Aunt Elspeth wrote the lyrics."

Joe laughed at Cleo's astonishment and dropped a kiss on the tip of her nose. "Now look at this," he said. Folding the manuscript over, he pointed to a note scrawled across the back.

" 'Ellie,' " Cleo read, " 'I thought your verse should be set to music. Hope this tune meets with your approval.' And it's signed, C.P." She stared at Joe, her eyes shining with discovery. "If this is authentic it could be valuable. Do you think it is authentic?"

"I'm no expert, honey, but the music sounds like Cole Porter, and the handwriting on the back is familiar."

"Then you think it's his?"

Joe shrugged and got to his feet. "What I think is that we should have the manuscript investigated by someone who's better informed than we are." On that note, Joe left the parlor. But he had given Cleo a lot to consider while he finished packing the records.

She was still in a mild state of shock fifteen minutes later when he returned to the parlor, a pair of champagne flutes in one hand, a portable cassette player in the other. He put the glasses and the cassette player on the coffee table, within easy reach of the love seat. Then he sat beside Cleo, took her in his arms, and kissed her as if they had been separated for weeks instead of minutes. Emotion thickened his voice as he said, "Even if the song isn't genuine, it'll be fun showing it to our grandkids."

"Grandkids!" she exclaimed softly. "Aren't you assuming an awful lot?"

Joe gave her a teasing grin. "I don't know, honey. You tell me. Would you like a formal proposal?"

"Yes!" she answered, and then she caught herself and smiled. "I guess I must be sentimental after all—"

He silenced her with a kiss. "Don't apologize, Cleo. Marriage is an important step, and I'm glad you're sentimental about it, because I am too. Truth is, I'd feel cheated if you didn't insist on a formal proposal. It'll give me the chance to show you how persuasive I can be."

Joe's mouth was sweet and sensuous, and his touch was heaven as his hands coasted from the nape of her neck to the base of her spine in a slow, cherishing caress.

"The party's not over after all," she murmured against his lips.

"If I have anything to say about it, it never will be," he replied in a husky murmur, pulling her into an embrace so deep, she could not distinguish where his body ended and hers began.

"The tape," she reminded him breathlessly.

"Right," Joe said.

He kept one arm around her while he slid Elspeth's

184

cassette into the player, and they sat close together, sipping champagne while they listened to the recording.

"They say experience is the best teacher," Elspeth began with surprising vigor, "and I believe it's true, which is why I staged this house party. I wanted to leave you something precious, Cleo, and given my limited resources, a treasure hunt was the best I could do.

"You've probably guessed there's a lesson to be learned from the last ten days, and it's this: In my ninety years, I've witnessed fire and flood, two world wars, recession and depression, prohibition and prosperity. I've seen the death of vaudeville, the birth of radio, the rise of movies and television, and the invention of the microchip. I've buried two husbands, divorced a third, and seen most of my friends and family die, and it seems to me, if I can live this long and experience all this and still believe in the fundamental goodness of my fellow man, then it must be safe for you to have a little faith.

"I wasn't good at showing how much I cared, but I love you, Cleo. Never doubt it. And Joe, if you're there— if this clambake worked out the way I planned, you damn well better be! Anyway, I just want to say I love you too, darlin'. You always made me feel as young as I wished I were."

"That's the end of the champagne," Joe whispered, taking Cleo's glass.

"I saved the cabernet," she said. "It's upstairs in my bedroom. With a little effort on your part, I might be persuaded to get it."

"I'll make the effort," Joe replied, his voice low and seductive, "but let's save the cabernet for tonight."

"Tonight," she repeated solemnly, so that it sounded like a vow. She tried to ask whether they would use the

185

cabernet for drinking or pouring, but the words were absorbed by Joe's mouth.

They were so engrossed with each other that neither of them heard Elspeth continue, her voice growing faint, "Be good to each other, my dear ones. If you're not, you never know—I just might come back to haunt you. I might come back anyway. Not that it's been all beer and skittles, mind you, but . . ."

There was a silence, a clearing of her throat, and then, almost inaudibly, Elspeth concluded, "Ah, God. If only I could do it all over again . . ."